INTRODUCTION BY
RICK RIORDAN

THE BLACK BOOK
OF BURIED SECRETS

SCHOLASTIC INC.

NEW YORK TORONTO LONDON AUCKLAND
SYDNEY MEXICO CITY NEW DELHI HONG KONG

Library of Congress Control Number: 2010929046
ISBN 978-0-545-28504-9
10 9 8 7 6 5 4 3 2 1   10 11 12 13 14

First edition, October 2010
Printed in the U.S.A.   23

Scholastic US: 557 Broadway · New York, NY 10012
Scholastic Canada: 604 King Street West · Toronto, ON · M5V 1E1
Scholastic New Zealand Limited: Private Bag 94407 · Greenmount, Manukau 2141
Scholastic UK Ltd.: Euston House · 24 Eversholt Street · London NW1 1DB

YOU HAVE BEEN CHOSEN AS
THE MOST LIKELY TO SUCCEED
IN THE GREATEST, MOST PERILOUS
UNDERTAKING OF ALL TIME —
A QUEST OF VITAL IMPORTANCE
TO THE CAHILL FAMILY
AND THE WORLD AT LARGE. . . .

INTERNATIONAL SIGNAL FLAGS

A B C D E
F G H I J
K L M N O
P Q R S T
U V W X Y
Z

HOW THE BLACK BOOK CAME TO BE

BY RICK RIORDAN, JANUS OPERATIVE

I was fairly sure I would not leave the meeting alive.

I came prepared with backup and concealed body armor, of course. Hidden in my sleeves were two quick-release canisters. With a flick of my wrists, I could release enough pepper spray to incapacitate downtown Manhattan.

Still . . . all seven agents had never been together in the same place before. We didn't trust one another, and we'd made powerful enemies by publishing our research on the 39 Clues. Any number of villains would love to have us all together to kidnap and interrogate . . . or worse. The meeting was a terrible idea. But it was my idea. We had no choice. Otherwise, the entire Cahill family might be wiped out.

The other six had already arrived. Wrapped in their trench coats, they milled about anxiously on the rooftop of Scholastic headquarters, which had been our cover these last eighteen months as we passed off our Cahill research as children's fiction. If only our work was fiction!

None of the other agents had yet registered my presence. Before I stepped out of the stairwell, I turned to my backup team — my own little army of secret weapons — lined up on the stairs. "Stay here," I told them. "I'll signal for you."

My backup team grumbled, anxious for combat, but they nodded in acknowledgment.

I stepped onto the roof, and the other six agents turned.

"Riordan," snarled Agent Korman. "You've got some nerve bringing us here."

With his shaven head, his shrewd eyes, his black clothes and combat boots, Agent Gordon Korman always reminded me of a Special Forces commando. For all I knew, he was one. He was a member of the Janus branch like me, but that didn't automatically make him an ally. I'd heard rumors that he'd evaded the entire Red Army after "liberating" secret Cahill files from Beijing. I'd heard he had spikes hidden in the tips of his combat boots, and once in Vienna he'd fended off six attackers with only his feet while finishing a Mozart concerto on the piano. I didn't want to find out if those rumors were true.

"Relax, Gordon," I said. "I'm not the enemy. We have a mutual problem."

Next to him, a man in a baseball cap laughed. "Got that right. I was almost captured on the way here. Is this some kind of trap?"

Agent Peter "the Great" Lerangis—another Janus— looked so easygoing with that friendly smile and twinkle in his eyes, but I knew better. This was the man who'd faced off against samurai and Zulu warriors in his search for the 39 Clues. He was more than just the world's foremost expert on Japanese calligraphy, African beadwork, and vintage baseball cards. He was a ruthless operative. At one point, the Tomas branch had put a four-million-dollar bounty on his baseball-capped head.

"Not a trap, Peter," I assured him. "We're facing a threat that could destroy all the Cahills. We have to work together."

"Ha!" The tallest agent of the group, Patrick Carman, stepped forward. He loomed over me, and I couldn't help retreating a little, because Patrick Carman, like most Lucians, has a talent for poison—needles, darts, cyanide-laced handkerchiefs. For all I knew, that smiley face button on his lapel squirted arsenic. And his time in Russia researching the Black Circle had no doubt added many new toxins to his arsenal. "News flash, Riordan," he said. "The hunt for the clues is over. Amy and Dan succeeded. Why should we work together anymore?"

"Because," said a woman's voice. "The hunt for the clues was only the beginning. Isn't that right?"

She stepped forward: Agent Jude Watson—at least that was one of her many names. Her fiery red hair curled around her face, and her scarf and thick-rimmed glasses made her look vaguely like an aviator—like Amelia Earhart, whom she'd worked so hard to track across the South Pacific. A golden scarab ring glittered on her right hand—no doubt a souvenir from her travels in Egypt. All the other agents turned toward her: out of fear or respect, it was hard to tell which. Agent Watson didn't appear menacing, but I'd never known anyone who wanted to cross her. She called herself an Ekaterina, though she commanded so much attention I wondered if perhaps she was one of the Cahill clan's master manipulators. Was it possible she could be a Madrigal?

"Riordan is correct about one thing," she continued.

"Now that the hunt is over, the Cahills face their greatest challenge ever. We're not the only ones who want the secret of our clan's power. Now that we have it, we must defend it against . . . the others."

The agents stirred apprehensively. Watson didn't need to speak the name of our enemy. We all knew whom she meant. It was the Cahills' darkest, most terrible nightmare—a half-whispered memory from our past, an adversary we wanted to believe was just a legend.

Next to Watson, a dark-haired woman in a cashmere coat shook her head. "But that's . . . impossible."

Agent Linda Sue Park did not scare easily. A Lucian master code breaker and weapons expert, she had searched the Caribbean for secrets more valuable than pirates' treasure. She could use forty-six different common household objects as deadly weapons. I'd seen her do more damage with a paper clip than most people could do with a machine gun. But at the mention of the Cahills' great enemy, Agent Park looked terrified.

"That's just a myth," she said hopefully, "a fable, a—"

"A lie?" said the seventh agent, Margaret Peterson Haddix. "It's no lie, Park. They're out there. And they're coming for us."

Haddix was the agent I knew the least, but I knew her reputation. She looked unassuming in her charcoal pantsuit and gold jewelry, her dark hair cut in a Cleopatra-style wedge. She might've been a journalist, a teacher, a mom—and, in fact, she'd been all three. But she was also an Ekaterina mastermind, an inventor who could build anything from a working steam-powered robot to a plan for global domination. She'd just returned from Ireland, where she'd been assigned to investigate the most critical part of the 39 Clues hunt—the ancient, final Gauntlet. Honestly, I think she got the assignment because she was the only one who could understand the Gauntlet's inner workings.

"I saw things in Ireland," she said. "Proof that our enemy is real. Riordan is right. We're all in very serious trouble."

Peter Lerangis straightened his baseball cap nervously. "But we've already written about the hunt for the clues. We've told the world about the Cahills. What else can we do?"

"A survival guide," suggested Jude Watson. "Pool our knowledge. That's what Riordan means. Isn't it?"

As usual, her intuition unnerved me. Was it possible she had a spy in my base of operations? I tried to keep calm, though. This was not going to be an easy negotiation.

"Yes," I agreed. "We have to prepare the branches for war. The only way to do that—"

"Share our branch secrets?" Park laughed incredulously. She looked at Patrick Carman, her fellow Lucian, for support. "The other branches can't seriously expect us Lucians to open up our files. We're light–years ahead of all of you!"

Gordon Korman snorted. "Oh, please. I've infiltrated your bases many times. You've got nothing."

"Why, you smug Janus—" Patrick Carman reached for the smiley face button on his lapel. He was probably a heartbeat away from spraying Agent Korman with some nasty concoction, but Agent Haddix stepped between them. "Stop it, you two," she ordered. "This is the kind of behavior that kept us from cooperating for five hundred years! We have to work together now, or we all perish."

Peter Lerangis shook his head in amazement. "So you're

serious? Haddix, you'd sign on to this? You'd put all Ekaterina secrets in writing for the world to see?"

Haddix pursed her lips. "I'm not saying I like it. But we have to cooperate. This only works if all the branches contribute."

"Forget it!" Korman said. "The Janus won't open their vaults for anyone. Besides, none of us are from the Tomas branch. Good luck getting them to play nice."

The project might've died right there. Looking around at the other six agents, I could feel their tension and paranoia— the distrust that had kept the Cahills apart for centuries. We might have cooperated enough to document the hunt for the 39 Clues, but uniting the Cahills to face an outside threat . . . that seemed impossible.

Fortunately, I had some secret weapons.

"We do have Tomas support," I announced. "In fact, we have a lot of it."

I raised my hand, and my backup team burst out of the shadows of the stairwell—a half dozen young agents in full ninja garb, their shirtsleeves emblazoned with the blue bear Tomas coat of arms.

My fellow author–agents gasped, but before they could make a move, the young Tomas operatives cartwheeled and flipped and rolled into position, their bo sticks, swords, and Taser guns ready for action. In a heartbeat, they had us surrounded.

Peter Lerangis threw down his cap and stomped on it. "I knew this was a trap! Riordan, you've sold us out to the Tomas? Traitor!"

"It's not a trap," I said. "These young agents—"

Jude Watson yelped in surprise. "The online agents!

They're players in the game!"

Once again, she'd gleaned the truth. When our hunt for the Clues had begun, we'd launched an online recruitment site to identify the most promising Cahill agents across the world. We called the 39 Clues site a "game," but it was deadly serious business. The top players in the game had quickly become even more knowledgeable about the 39 Clues than I was.

"We've never been in this alone," I told my fellow authors. "From the start, the online agents have been at our side, leading the hunt. Amy and Dan wouldn't have succeeded without them. I knew we'd never reach an agreement on a survival guide without Tomas help, so I took the liberty of contacting their top-scoring players."

Patrick Carman's eyes widened with sudden understanding. The Tomas commando standing in front of him couldn't have been more than a teenager and was much shorter than Carman, but Carman backed away in a panic.

"My God!" he said. "You're—you're WiseSaladin1!"

The commando nodded gravely, acknowledging the online alias.

"That's right," I said. "At last count, WiseSaladin1 had over four thousand points in the game. And here we have BaseballDragon1, OnyxEagle7, and—"

"All right!" Gordon Korman looked pale, his forehead beaded with sweat. "We get it, Riordan. You brought in the elite Tomas troops. What do you want? Just please, no Tasers!"

I gestured to the Tomas commandos, and they lowered their weapons.

"They're not here to fight," I said. "They're here to help.

They've pledged to open up Tomas secrets, as long as the other branches do the same. I'd urge us all to cooperate."

Haddix seemed to recover first. She took a deep breath, though she still looked unnerved.

"So," she said. "We all agree to share our branch secrets. We collect them into one volume and publish them for the benefit of all Cahill operatives."

"THE BLACK BOOK OF BURIED SECRETS," Watson suggested. "That's what we call it."

Park glanced nervously at the commando on her left, probably wondering if she could disarm the young agent before getting bonked with a bo stick. Apparently, she didn't like her chances.

"Very well," she said. "A BLACK BOOK—the ultimate source of Cahill knowledge. I suppose I can see the advantage. With power like that, collected in a single volume—we could sell it for millions!"

"No," Haddix said. "We make it available to everyone—treat it like a regular book, just as we did with the 39 Clues volumes. Once the BLACK BOOK is open to all Cahills, it could give us the knowledge we need to defeat the enemy."

"Or it could doom us," Gordon Korman grumbled. "We'd be giving away our secrets, trusting the other branches. What if it leads to more infighting?" He glanced suspiciously at OnyxEagle7.

"We have to try," I said. "The enemy is preparing for war. We have to combine our knowledge to fight them. Our choice is simple: publish or perish."

One by one, the agents nodded. No one was comfortable sharing so much secret information, but they knew I was right. The BLACK BOOK was our only chance. And the fact that

I had an army of Tomas backing me up probably didn't hurt, either.

So I survived the meeting. An agreement was struck. THE BLACK BOOK OF BURIED SECRETS was created.

This is the book you now hold in your hands.

Within these pages, you will find everything you need to become the ultimate Cahill operative. You will learn the secret locations of branch headquarters around the world—even for the Madrigals. The identities of each branch's key operatives are revealed. Personnel dossiers have been opened for the first time in Cahill history, so you know exactly who works for which branch, and what abilities they have.

You will learn about each branch's top secret arsenals of weapons and gadgets. Nothing has been held back. Once you read this book, you will have the combined knowledge of all the Cahill branches.

Remember: We are risking everything to put this information in your hands. Learn it well. We are counting on you.

We hope this will be enough to equip you for the battles to come, but make no mistake. The Cahills may have survived the hunt for the 39 Clues, but our greatest challenge is yet to come. Keep this BLACK BOOK OF SECRETS close at all times. The enemy is approaching.

DESTROY AFTER READING

MADRIGALS

MADRIGALS AT A GLANCE

For centuries, the word *Madrigal* sent shivers down Cahill spines. No one was sure who they were, or why they would emerge from the shadows to attack Clue hunters—especially those on the verge of a major breakthrough. In 1826 Russian Lucians led by Grand Duke Constantine came desperately close to assembling all 39 Clues. The night before an agent was due to return from a mission with one of the last Clues, Constantine heard a terrible crash, followed by screams. It was the Madrigals. By the time Constantine reached his hidden lab in the basement, the Madrigals were gone, and his life's work was destroyed. Surrounded by shattered glass and smoldering papers was a large M burned into the floor.

SECRET HISTORY

Until recently, none of the other Cahills knew that the Madrigals were actually a fifth branch of the family, descended from Madeleine Cahill, the youngest daughter of Gideon and Olivia. Gideon died before he knew his wife was expecting a fifth child. He was killed in a fire that destroyed the laboratory where he hid the secrets of the 39 Clues. Gideon's death tore the Cahill family apart. Two of the children believed that the eldest, Luke, was responsible for the fire. By the time Madeleine was born, her brothers and sisters had left Ireland, leaving her mother alone on their small island in the Irish Sea.

Olivia was heartbroken by how her children's obsession with Clues had shattered her family, and she realized that the power of the 39 Clues was too dangerous for any individual to possess. She raised Madeleine to believe in both the importance of uniting the family . . . and keeping any one of her siblings from collecting all the Clues.

STRATEGY

While the Lucians, Ekaterinas, Janus, and Tomas competed for world domination, the Madrigals worked to maintain balance. They knew that if any one branch found the Clues, the power they unlocked could be devastating.

For the past five centuries, the Madrigals have monitored the other Cahills, often sending double agents to infiltrate the branches. Even the star of the Lucian branch, Napoleon Bonaparte, had no idea that one of his top advisers was actually a Madrigal spy. Whenever a group came too close to assembling all the Clues, the Madrigals would step in, doing whatever was necessary to keep this explosive power out of reach. In most cases, this meant destroying strongholds or burning precious documents. However, in extreme situations, the Madrigals were willing to spill blood to prevent the creation of an all-powerful Cahill.

FOUNDERS

For the past five hundred years, innocent people have suffered as Cahills toppled governments, ignited wars, and developed new weapons in order to become the first to find the Clues. Part of the Madrigal philosophy is to counteract the damage of the Clue hunt by helping the world at large. Throughout history, Madrigals have founded organizations like the Red Cross and other groups devoted to promoting peace, health, and harmony.

STRONGHOLDS

There are two official Madrigal strongholds, one on a deserted island in the Irish Sea and another on Easter Island in the South Pacific, hidden underneath one of its mysterious stone statues. However, a number of Madrigal organizations have become unofficial strongholds, such as United Nations headquarters in New York City.

CREST

The Madrigals use the Cahill "C" as their symbol in the hope that someday the warring branches of the family will be united once again. When they want to send a message of fear, they use the Madrigal "M." Just the sight of it has been known to send the bravest Clue hunters off screaming.

MADRIGAL
FOUNDERS

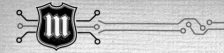

In the other branches of the Cahill family, membership is automatically passed from parents to children. However, Madrigals have to earn the right to join their branch. They must demonstrate bravery, compassion, and the ability to stand up for their beliefs under the most challenging circumstances. Madrigal founders include:

HOPE CAHILL	FREDERICK DOUGLASS
ARTHUR TRENT	ANNE BONNY
GRACE CAHILL	NANNY SHARPE
AMELIA EARHART	WILLIAM SHAKESPEARE
FLORENCE NIGHTINGALE	WALT WHITMAN
ABIGAIL ADAMS	CAMILLE WIZARD
HARRIET TUBMAN	MOTHER TERESA

HOPE CAHILL (1960–2001)

Hope Cahill didn't learn about the Clues until she was twelve. She had no idea that her mother, Grace, had a secret reason for filling Hope's days with Chinese and Swahili classes, karate lessons, and explosives training. However, Hope eventually became committed to the Madrigal cause and chose to study archaeology in college. As an archaeologist, she could travel the world without attracting attention and gain the skills needed to unearth Clues that had been hidden for centuries.

At first, Hope viewed the Clue hunt as the ultimate adventure. She found her first Clue while working on a dig near Petra, Jordan, and couldn't stop grinning for days. The thrill of discovery was addictive. After she married Arthur Trent, the handsome mathematician she met in Istanbul, he began traveling with Hope. Their Clue-hunting missions felt like an extended honeymoon—a honeymoon that involved digging up graves, breaking into museums, and avoiding assassins' bullets.

However, after Amy and Dan were born, Hope started to think differently about the hunt. The dangerous missions that once left her exhilarated now made her anxious. Hope began to worry about what would happen to her children if she and Arthur were killed. Yet at the same time, the hunt grew increasingly urgent. The more Hope learned about the other branches, the more committed she became to keeping the Clues out of their hands. After witnessing Isabel Kabra kill a museum guard in South Africa, Hope came to an agonizing realization—it was more important to make the world safe for her children than to keep herself alive to raise them.

ARTHUR TRENT (1959–2001)

The Cahills believe that they've kept their existence secret. However, there are a few people who know about the 39 Clues—the Vespers. Arthur Trent was born into a family with close ties to this secret organization. He was raised to believe that the Cahills were weaklings and that the power of the Clues belonged in Vesper hands. It wasn't a coincidence that Arthur was working in Turkey at the same time as Hope. He had been sent to find her and ordered to make

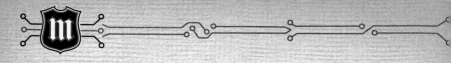

her fall in love with him. However, when Arthur actually met his beautiful target, something happened. He was enchanted by her intelligence, her kindness, and the way her nose twitched when she laughed.

In Turkey, Arthur learned some terrifying information about the Vespers. He realized that he needed to cut his ties to the organization, although the act would put him in danger for the rest of his life. Before he proposed, Arthur told Hope the truth about his background, but Hope already knew. William McIntyre's spies had been following him for months.

Although Arthur was never granted official Madrigal status, he become one of their top agents and was completely devoted to the cause. That's why, on the night of the fire, he ran to his study instead of escaping with his children. The growing flames and clouds of smoke couldn't distract him from his goal, although they ultimately claimed his life.

FLORENCE NIGHTINGALE (1820–1910)

Florence Nightingale was a British woman who served as a nurse in the Crimean War. When she realized that more soldiers were dying from disease than from battle wounds, Nightingale developed a number of methods for improving hygiene. As a result, she saved countless lives and revolutionized the nursing profession. After earning her Madrigal status, Nightingale became committed to the hunt, using her opportunities for travel to hunt Clues around Europe.

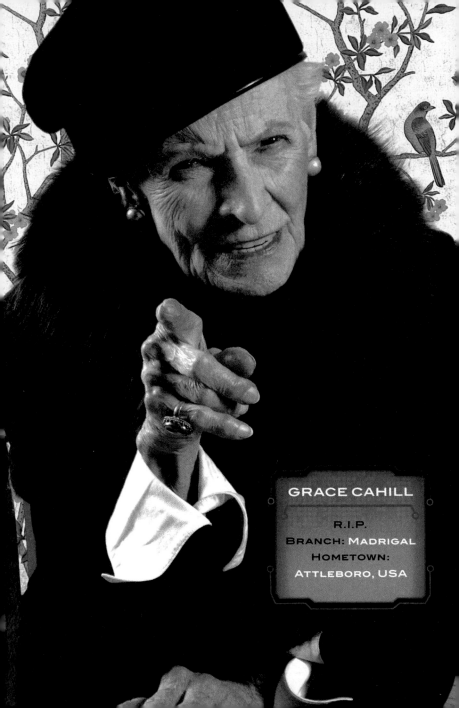

GRACE CAHILL

R.I.P.
BRANCH: MADRIGAL
HOMETOWN:
ATTLEBORO, USA

Founder Archives: Grace Cahill

It was as if someone had thrown a blanket over London. Black material covered all the windows, cars careened through the night without headlights, and residents were forbidden from smoking outside. A German bomber flying overhead might use the red glow of a cigarette as a target.

Yet as she and Beatrice hurried through the darkness, fifteen-year-old Grace Cahill felt a wave of excitement pass through her, leaving a delicious tingle in its wake. She'd take London over Massachusetts any day, even with the threat of an air raid. She thrilled at the feeling of her saddle shoes pounding the pavement. Young ladies at Miss Harper's School for Girls were not supposed to run.

Grace felt like a prisoner who had broken out of her shackles and was just beginning to regain sensation in her limbs. Sophomore year at boarding school had been a numbing stream of etiquette classes and priggish dorm monitors. All that had kept her from sneaking off in the middle of the night had been her training. The books she'd devoured about Egyptian history. The hours in the gym practicing back handsprings on the balance beam.

When the Madrigals had called her, she'd been ready.

Grace and Beatrice skidded to a stop as the shadowy outline of the Tower of London came into view.

"I can't believe we're actually doing this," Beatrice muttered. Even in the darkness, she appeared pale.

Grace glanced at her watch and grinned. "Come on. It's time to go."

The two girls ran for a few more yards and then pressed themselves flat against the wall just outside the gates. "Only one more minute," Grace whispered.

"How do you know?"

"The Ceremony of the Keys is performed at nine fifty-three every night. The tradition goes back seven hundred years."

"Where are all the other people?" Beatrice asked.

"The Tower's been closed to the public since the war started."

"What will they do if they catch us?" Beatrice had started shaking, even though the summer night was warm.

Grace grinned again. "We're not going to find out."

The sound of stomping boots made her turn. A line of soldiers from the Tower of London guard stood in front of the gate as a man in an old-fashioned black-and-red uniform—the chief Yeoman Warder—approached. Grace held her breath as the ritual locking of the Tower of London began.

"Who comes there?" shouted one of the soldiers.

"The keys," the Yeoman Warder replied.

"Whose keys?"

"King George's keys."

"Pass King George's keys. All's well."

Grace grabbed Beatrice's arm. That was their sign.

But Beatrice wouldn't budge. She simply stared at the backs of the soldiers as they marched through the gates. "Come on," Grace hissed. "We need to go now."

Beatrice's eyes were wide. "I can't do this," she whispered.

Grace took a deep breath. She knew how to handle her older sister. "Fine," she said nonchalantly. "Then I'll go by myself." She took a step.

Grace heard Beatrice groan and shuffle forward. "You know I can't let you do that."

Grace turned and smiled. "Then let's go."

As they ran, Grace reached into her bag and pulled out a grappling hook. Next to her, Beatrice was clutching a coil of rope. Grace's heart was pounding and her lungs were taking in greedy gulps of the night air. Despite the frantic pace, she could identify the movement of each body part as the adrenaline switched them into high gear. She had never felt so alive.

They slid to a stop in front of a building Grace recognized from their mission briefing. The Salt Tower. Grace tied Beatrice's rope to her hook, swung it in a large circle above her head, and, with a well-practiced flick, sent it flying.

There was a clank as the hook caught the iron window bars. "You first," she whispered to Beatrice, shoving the rope into her hands. Beatrice didn't move. "Go!" Grace said, a little louder. Her sister gritted her teeth, grabbed the rope, and began to climb.

Once they were inside, Grace switched on her flashlight and shone it around the dark, damp room. The stone walls were covered with writing. Her pulse racing, Grace stepped forward to take a closer look. Centuries of prisoners had carved messages into the walls. Vows of revenge. Farewells to loved ones. She shivered, thinking of the countless condemned men and women who had spent their final nights in this cell.

"Grace," Beatrice whispered. "Come look." Her flashlight beam was also focused on one of the carvings, but this one was an image. A snake. Grace pulled a hammer and a chisel out of her bag and began tapping along the edge of the stone. When she finished, she gently pried it out of the wall, revealing a compartment behind. Inside was a simple wooden bowl filled with tiny white crystals. Salt? No, it couldn't be that easy. Salt hidden in the Salt Tower. She grabbed the bowl and poured some of the contents into a vial, which she sealed and tossed into her bag. She slid the stone back into the wall and grabbed Beatrice's arm. "Let's go."

They ran out of the cell, up a spiral staircase, and climbed through a trapdoor onto the roof. Grace looked at her watch and then craned her neck to scan the sky. They had to be on their way.

Her heart thudded against her chest, a metronome setting the beat for the chorus of thoughts running through her head. *They have to come. They have to come. They have to come.*

She became so fixated on that rhythm that, at first, she didn't notice the other set of pounding noises. The rapid beat of heavy footsteps. She glanced over the edge of the roof and saw two lines of men running down the alley toward the Salt Tower. Their red snake badges shone faintly in the moonlight. The Lucians were coming for them.

Grace turned and saw her sister gasping for air. Her breathing had become rapid and shallow. She was hyperventilating. "Breathe," Grace commanded, grabbing Beatrice's shoulders. "You have to breathe."

"They're coming. They're coming," Beatrice wheezed, her eyes wide with terror. The two lines of men disappeared. They had entered the tower and must be climbing the stairs.

Grace ran to the edge. Was there any chance of surviving if they jumped? A noise from above made her spin around. A black plane was flying toward them, a ladder swinging from the hatch.

Beatrice screamed. The trapdoor opened, and the first of the Lucian guards sprang onto the roof. He glanced up at the approaching aircraft and shouted something to the others, but Grace couldn't make it out above the roar of the engine. The ladder swung by Beatrice. She leaped and grabbed one of the rungs. "Grace!" she screamed as the ladder flew toward her sister. Grace would only have one chance. Five men were running toward her, removing guns from their holsters.

Grace jumped and grabbed on to the ladder, clutching Beatrice as they swung back and forth in the air. Slowly, they began to rise as the Madrigal agents pulled them in. The girls collapsed on the floor.

"Whoo-hoo!" Grace yelled as one of the agents tried to wrap her in a blanket. "We did it! That was unbelievable!" She turned to Beatrice. Another agent was fitting an oxygen mask over her sister's face. Beatrice hadn't stopped shaking.

"Beatrice." Grace took a step forward. "Are you OK?"

Beatrice mumbled something that Grace couldn't hear. She took another step. "Are you OK?" she repeated.

Beatrice pulled the mask away from her mouth. Her face was chalky and her lips had a bluish tint. "I'm out," she sobbed. "I'm never doing anything like this again." ❖

8 11 16 6   22 10 7   21 3 8 7

6 7 18 17 21 11 22   4 17 26

KEY: A = 12/4

MADELEINE CAHILL (1507–?)

Months before she was born, Madeleine Cahill's family was destroyed. Her father, Gideon, was killed in a fire that broke out in his lab.Two of her siblings, Thomas and Katherine, suspected their sly older brother, Luke, of sabotage. Enraged by the accusation, Luke fled the family home, followed by his favorite sister, Jane. Thomas and Katherine left shortly after to hide their Clues somewhere Luke would never find them. Their mother, Olivia, was left alone on the Cahills' island off the coast of Ireland.

Madeleine was born to a heartbroken woman who spent the rest of her life mourning the loss of her family. However, Olivia knew she had to remain strong for her youngest daughter. She worked hard to build a life for them on the island and devoted herself to Madeleine's education. Olivia raised her daughter to value bravery, generosity, and compassion. Most important, she taught Madeleine that it was crucial to heal the rift that had destroyed the Cahill family.

Olivia made Madeleine swear that she would do whatever necessary to keep her siblings from collecting all 39 Clues. Until they learned to trust again, Luke, Katherine, Thomas, and Jane would use the power of the Clues to destroy one another. If that wasn't enough of a challenge, Olivia also charged Madeleine with the task of protecting Gideon's Clues and an ancient gold ring from Damien Vesper, a former friend who became Gideon's most dangerous rival. Olivia knew she was asking a great deal of her youngest daughter, but she had no idea that the Madrigals would spend the next 500 years making countless sacrifices in pursuit of these goals.

WILLIAM SHAKESPEARE (1564–1616)

William Shakespeare was an English poet and playwright considered by many to be the greatest writer of all time. Yet Shakespeare was not a member of the Janus branch. He was the grandson of Madeleine Cahill and became a powerful Madrigal agent.

Non-Cahill scholars have always been puzzled by Shakespeare's "lost years," the period of his life when he seems to vanish from all records. But the Madrigals know the truth. Shakespeare was off looking for the other branches' Clues. After he married, Shakespeare abandoned the hunt and devoted himself to his art—but his writing was always inspired by his heartbreak over the Cahill rift.

Shakespeare wrote a lot about family feuds, from *Romeo and Juliet* to *King Lear*. Other plays dealt with bloodthirsty leaders, such as *Julius Caesar* and *Macbeth*. However, while Shakespeare feared the consequences of the Clue hunt, he still hoped for peace. He even secretly penned a play about the reunion of the Cahill family—*Love's Labour's Won*.

While Shakespeare wrote about some serious issues, he also had a genius for comedy and a flair for insults. It takes a true master of the English language to invent zingers like "thou lump of foul deformity."

Shakespeare also hid several Clues in his plays. The actual number is one of the last remaining Madrigal secrets, but quite a few have been uncovered, including Thyme, Clover, Bone, Lily, Rosemary, and Blood.

MADRIGAL
AGENTS

Over the past few years, Madrigal membership has declined drastically. After a careless mistake allowed an imposter into the branch, the Madrigals changed their screening process. Their requirements became much stricter, making it difficult to find qualified candidates. The Madrigals can't afford to take any chances. Members of the branch are responsible for protecting the most valuable secrets on earth. They know that the fate of the world is in their hands.

CURRENT MADRIGAL AGENTS INCLUDE:
AMY CAHILL
DAN CAHILL
NELLIE GOMEZ
WILLIAM MCINTYRE
FISKE CAHILL
SALADIN
EMILY MARTELLA
NATALIYA RUSLANOVNA RADOVA (LUCIAN DOUBLE AGENT)
ROBERT BARDSLEY (TOMAS DOUBLE AGENT)
~~ANA KOSARA~~

ROBERT BARDSLEY

Music professor Robert Bardsley was born a Tomas and was an active Clue hunter in his youth. However, he became frustrated by his branch's constant fighting and disgusted by their willingness to hurt people who got in their way. He eventually quit the Tomas, vowing to abstain from the hunt altogether. Years later, his close friend Grace tried to recruit him for the Madrigals. At first, Robert was horrified. He had heard only terrible things about the Madrigals and couldn't believe that his dear friend could be one. Even after she told him the truth about her branch, he refused to

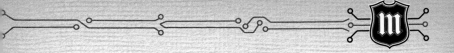

join. He had seen too much hate, too much bloodshed. He wanted nothing to do with Clues and instead devoted himself to music and teaching. However, when the hunt led Amy and Dan to South Africa, Robert knew it was his duty to help Grace's grandchildren. After heroically rescuing Amy and Dan, the Madrigals once again offered to make Robert a member. This time, he accepted. Watching Isabel Kabra try to kill the children made him realize the seriousness of the hunt and the vital importance of the Madrigal cause.

SALADIN

Grace's cat, Saladin, might appear to be a spoiled pet, but he's actually an accomplished honorary agent in his own right. Grace trained her Egyptian Mau to sneak into buildings too dangerous for her to enter, like the Lucian stronghold in Moscow. She even developed cat-size surveillance equipment for him to carry on his secret missions. Saladin was happy to help, even if it required him to don scuba gear and swim. No feat is too great as long as there is a reward of red snapper at the end.

EMILY MARTELLA

Emily is a physician working for Doctors Without Borders, an organization that brings medical aid to countries threatened by war and other disasters around the world. Although her work keeps her very busy, Emily is also a top agent. When the Madrigals learned that the Tomas were only a few Clues away from re-creating the Ekaterina serum, they sent Emily on

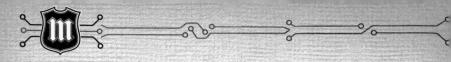

an urgent mission to the Bermuda Triangle. Having earned her scuba certification as part of her Madrigal training, she located and disabled a Tomas submarine looking for the hidden Ekat base. Not only did she keep the Tomas from finding the Clue, but she prevented the chaos that would have erupted when the Ekats discovered they were robbed. Conflict between the branches had already resulted in too many innocent deaths.

WILLIAM McINTYRE

William McIntyre was born to a Madrigal mother and a non-Cahill father. At eighteen, he joined the elite Navy Seals before attending law school, where he graduated at the top of his class. When Grace Cahill was looking for a new lawyer, she was intrigued by William's special qualifications. Some people might wonder why a lawyer needs to know how to jump out of a plane or defuse an underwater bomb, but Grace had unique requirements. She needed someone who could both draw up a contract and break her out of a foreign prison. William was granted Madrigal status and became one of Grace's closest friends and advisers. He was responsible for forging the fake passports Amy and Dan used

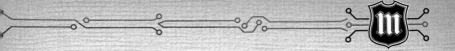

to travel to Russia, and for opening their Visa Gold card. Ever since Dan found that out, he's been bugging William for another.

ANA KOSARA

The branch leadership was thrilled to grant Ana Kosara Madrigal status. A teacher, political activist, and member of the Ekaterina branch, Ana passed the Madrigal test with flying colors. The Madrigal leaders were particularly impressed with her efforts to fund orphanages in her native Bulgaria. However, soon after Ana joined the branch, strange things started happening. Top secret documents disappeared. Madrigal agents were unable to complete simple missions. It was as if the other branches knew their plans ahead of time. The leadership launched an investigation and made a shocking discovery. Ana was an imposter. Her Cahill lineage was real, but her qualifications were not. She had lied about her teaching experience. She had faked the orphanages. It was all part of a plan to infiltrate the Madrigals on behalf of the Vespers—a secret organization that has been trying to sabotage the Cahills for the past five hundred years. Ana was expelled and the Madrigals drastically changed their screening process, but the damage was done.

Keyword: Protect

AMY CAHILL

AGE: 14
BRANCH: MADRIGAL
HOMETOWN:
BOSTON, USA

From: **Amy Cahill** › Info

To: **Fiske Cahill** › Info

Dear Uncle Fiske,

Sorry I missed your call. We're not allowed to use cell phones at school. I read the rule book last night to make up for missing orientation.

Dan said I need to relax. He told me there was probably a rule against two kids landing a helicopter on top of Mount Everest, too. I explained that since Everest is on the border of Tibet and Nepal, no one has jurisdiction over the summit. Then Dan said that someone who just saved the world should be less of a supernerd. I told him that someone who just saved the world should stop wearing Pokemon underwear.

First period (World History) was a little weird. Mrs. Withers asked me where I'd been for the past three weeks. I did what you told me and said that I had been "taking care of a sick relative." (It's kinda true. Dan's definitely sick in the head.) She sighed and said that I better catch up fast because it wasn't fair to hold the other students back. It was awful. Everyone was staring at me and my cheeks started to burn—I knew they were turning red.

But then during class, Mrs. Withers asked a question about Shaka Zulu's battle strategy. I guess she had assigned reading on him earlier. No one knew the answer. I said that Shaka arranged his warriors in a buffalo horn formation, allowing him to overpower his enemies even if they had superior weaponry. Mrs. Withers just stared at me until the bell rang a few seconds later.

I should go because I have a ton of homework to do.

Love, Amy

P.S. You'll have to meet with Dan's principal when you get back. He got in trouble for doing ninja moves in class. Don't worry. This happens all the time.

DAN CAHILL

AGE: 11
BRANCH: MADRIGAL
HOMETOWN:
BOSTON, USA

CAHILL, DANIEL

PERMANENT · RECORD
OFFICE OF THE PRINCIPAL

ADAMS MIDDLE SCHOOL
DISCIPLINARY RECORD

NAME: DANIEL CAHILL   **GUARDIAN:** FISKE CAHILL

DATE: October 4th   **CLASS:** Homeroom   **TEACHER:** Mr. Garcia

INCIDENT: Disrupted class. Threatened teacher.

REPORT: Mr. Garcia asked Dan why he missed the first three weeks of school. Dan replied, "It's top secret. If I told you, someone in my family might try to kill you. But I'd stop them. I learned wushu from Shaolin monks!" Dan then jumped up from his desk to demonstrate. His kick broke the table with the aquarium on it. Herbert the goldfish is in critical condition. Dan was sent to the principal's office.

DATE: October 4th   **CLASS:** History   **TEACHER:** Mrs. Travis

INCIDENT: Disrupted class. Talked back to teacher.

REPORT: When Mrs. Travis announced an essay topic on Benjamin Franklin, Dan asked if he could write about Franklin's interest in farts. She was appalled and said that Franklin had never discussed "flatulence." Dan replied that Franklin had written a joke essay, proposing to study different kinds of farts. Mrs. Travis told Dan that he was "disrespecting one of our most revered founders." Dan grew angry and said that she was ignoring his greatest accomplishment. Dan was sent to the principal's office.

DATE: October 4th   **CLASS:** Music   **TEACHER:** Mr. Haverford

INCIDENT: Disrupted class. Endangered students.

REPORT: Mr. Haverford was explaining how the composer Mozart died bankrupt. Dan interrupted the lecture to explain that Mozart had spent all his money "importing crazy materials from around the world, like tungsten." Mr. Haverford told Dan that he was wrong. Dan replied, "It's true! I even have a model of the exact samurai swords he wanted to buy. Look!" He then produced a sword from his backpack and began waving it in the air. The sword was confiscated. Dan was sent to the principal's office.

AGENT UPDATE: Amy and Dan Cahill

After surviving explosions, poisonous snake attacks, and a leaky submarine, Amy Cahill did not want to die on the Mass Turnpike.

"Nellie!" she shouted as their au pair swerved to pass yet another car. "There's no one chasing us anymore. You can keep it under ninety for a while!"

"Caught in a bad romance. Whoaaa-oh-ooooh!" Nellie wailed along to the XM radio blaring from the enormous speakers.

"Nellie!"

"What?" She looked over and saw Amy glowering. "Sorry, kiddo." Nellie smiled sheepishly. "But this bad boy has a need for speed." She patted the steering wheel fondly. When Amy didn't respond, Nellie frowned slightly. "Are you okay? I mean, I know this trip is going to be—"

"I'm fine," Amy interrupted. She forced a smile.

"Can I uncover my ears now?" Dan called from the back, where he was reclined across the leather seat. "Has Nellie stopped her Lady Gag Me impression?"

"Fine, so singing isn't one of my many talents," Nellie said. "Now, ask me to find a restaurant that serves Mongolian-Brazilian fusion, and I've got you covered. Oooh! I bet the GPS thingy here could do it. Let's see . . ." Nellie took one hand off the steering wheel and began fiddling with the touch-screen navigation system.

"Nellie!" Amy yelped as their car started drifting toward the concrete median. "Focus!"

"Chill out, Amy," Dan shouted over the music. "Nothing can happen to us in"—he lowered his voice so it sounded like a movie trailer—"The Madrigalator."

Amy rolled her eyes. "The Madrigalator" was what Dan had named their new car—the enormous SUV Fiske had bought them when they got back to Boston. Amy had wanted a Prius, but Fiske insisted on the armored gas guzzler. "Isabel Kabra might be locked up," he had said, "but there are still people out there who want to hurt you."

Of course, he hadn't considered the danger of giving Nellie a two-ton death machine with access to almost every song in the world.

At the next exit, Nellie pulled off the highway and turned on to a tree-lined road. The gas stations and convenience stores disappeared. After a few miles, the road narrowed and they were driving under a canopy of rust- and copper-colored leaves. Dan sat up. Nellie turned off the music unprompted.

They drove for a few minutes before Nellie broke the silence. "I can't believe Beatrice never took you guys here," she said softly. "That's just cruel."

Amy glanced back at Dan. He never missed an opportunity to make fun of their great-aunt. But this time, he said nothing.

They rounded a bend and tall iron gates came into view. CRESTWOOD CEMETERY. Nellie turned in to the driveway and parked next to the caretaker's building. No one moved. After a few long moments, Nellie unfastened her seat belt, reached over, and squeezed Amy's hand. "Let's go say hi to your parents, kiddo."

They climbed the same hill Amy had trudged up seven years before. She remembered having to hold Dan's hand tightly because the grass had been damp, and he kept slipping in his tiny, brand-new dress shoes.

Hope's and Arthur's graves were side by side. The stones had faded slightly, and grass had grown over the dirt mounds.

HOPE CAHILL	ARTHUR TRENT
1960 — 2001	1959 — 2001
FRIEND, MOTHER, EXPLORER	TEACHER, FATHER, ADVENTURER

Amy took a few steps and knelt down, ignoring the dampness from the grass seeping through the knees of her jeans. She reached forward and brushed her hand against Hope's headstone. No one had let her near the grave during the funeral. She hadn't even been able to see over the line of black-clad bodies in front of her. "Hi, Mom," she said softly, tracing the letters. Amy closed her eyes. After the fire, she used to stay awake long into the night, convinced that if she was completely quiet, she might be able to hear her parents. She pushed her hand against the stone, feeling the cold spread to her fingers. After a moment, she exhaled. She hadn't realized she had been holding her breath.

Amy reached into her pocket and pulled out the bead of amber they'd found in Russia. She placed it in the groove between the stone and the grass. "I think you were still looking for this one."

Beside her, Dan was sprinkling a packet of mace next to Arthur's headstone. "I wish you could've been with us in Jamaica," he said. "You would've liked Lester."

Amy ran her fingers along one of the decorations on her mother's headstone, a carving of a rose. There was only one, which almost made it look like it had grown out of the stone. "Mom loved roses," Amy told Dan as he came over to sit next to her. "Dad would always bring them home."

Dan reached up and touched the carving. "Something's different here," he said.

"You were four at the funeral. Of course it looks different."

"No," he said, staring at the rose curiously. "I mean, it looks different from the rest of the decorations." He traced his fingers along it and then leaned forward to press his ear against the headstone.

Amy sighed. The hunt had made them paranoid. They couldn't even visit their parents' graves like normal people. "Dan," she started. "We can't—"

"Hold on," he interrupted. He looked over at Amy. "I think I found something." Before Amy had a chance to stop him, he pressed his hand against the rose and pushed. There was a strange clicking sound, like gears turning, and a metal lever emerged from the side of the tombstone.

"Whooooa." Amy heard Nellie whistle behind them. "Just when you think you've seen it all."

Dan looked at Amy. "This doesn't usually happen, right?"

"No. Well, not in most families."

Dan reached out to touch the lever. "Wait," Amy said, grabbing his arm. The Clue hunt was over. They didn't need whatever was hidden inside the grave. She thought of the passports they'd found that linked their parents to a murder. The agonizing weeks she'd spent convinced that Hope and Arthur were killers. She didn't want to know any more secrets.

Dan looked at her. She could tell he knew what she was thinking. "We can't go back to how it was before. The hunt was part of them. We know that now." He paused. "But that doesn't mean they loved us any less."

Amy smiled. "You might be a dweeb, but you're a wise dweeb."

He nodded seriously. "It's all from Yoda." He extended his arm again. "Ready." Amy nodded.

Dan pulled the lever. This time, a small vial rose out of the top of the gravestone. It was filled with a clear liquid. *Vinegar*, Amy thought. One of the Clues. Dan reached forward and grabbed the vial. There were letters etched into the glass. Another code.

LFFQ HJEFPOT HPME SJOH TBGF

But this time, they wouldn't have to rush to the airport as soon as they cracked it. They could just go home. As Dan ran over to Nellie to show her their find, Amy leaned forward and whispered the two words she'd been waiting seven years to say. "Good-bye, Mom." ❖

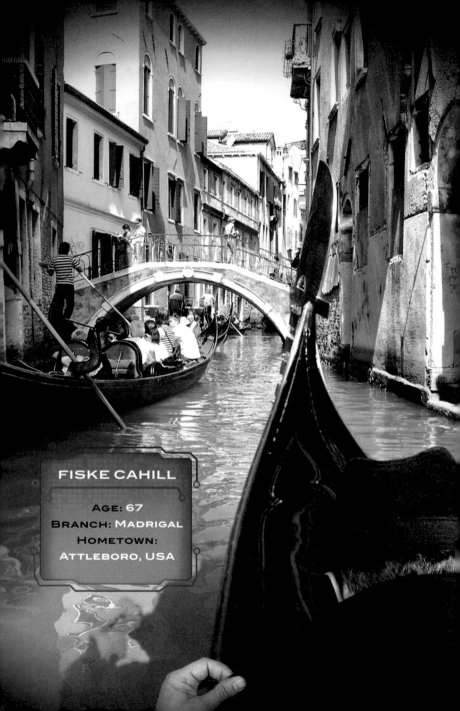

FISKE CAHILL

AGE: 67
BRANCH: MADRIGAL
HOMETOWN:
ATTLEBORO, USA

FISKE CAHILL (THE MAN IN BLACK)

Growing up, Fiske Cahill wasn't the "I get nervous before giving book reports" kind of shy. He was "talking to strangers makes me feel like my ears are on fire and there's a hyperactive frog tap-dancing in my stomach" kind of shy. Even worse, Fiske had a terrible stutter, which made it difficult for even the nicest, most patient people to understand him. And, in the Cahill family, not everyone was nice.

Fiske's shyness made him a target. His relatives thought that he'd be easier to bully than Grace, but that he'd know more about the Clues than Beatrice. At Cahill gatherings, agents from other branches would press Fiske for information. By the time he was in middle school, cars were following him home. The Janus even sent a child actor to spy on Fiske, pretending to be his friend so he could snoop around Fiske's bedroom.

While Grace understood Fiske's shyness, it infuriated their father, James. He expected Fiske to play a major role in the Cahill world—leading meetings and dangerous missions. By the time Fiske left for art school, the pressure had become unbearable. He was unsure who was a fellow student and who was a Cahill spy. Finally, Fiske made a desperate decision. He disappeared, and spent nearly fifty years in hiding.

Fiske was never at ease with his decision. Still, he refused Grace's pleas to help until just weeks before her death, when he returned to oversee the competition—and to keep Amy and Dan safe.

After almost five decades away from his family, Fiske is making up for lost time as Amy and Dan's guardian. Yet despite the pleasure of book shopping with Amy or watching ninja movies with Dan, Fiske can't really relax. He knows that it's just a matter of time before this new peace is shattered.

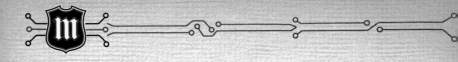

NELLIE GOMEZ

Nellie never thought it was strange that she went to flying lessons while her friends played soccer, or that she won five scholarships to study foreign languages. And when her father signed her up for defensive driving lessons, she figured it was because of that time she paid too much attention to the cute boy in the next car and not enough attention to the red light. Nellie had no idea that her driving skills would one day save her life . . . and the lives of two kids charged with protecting the world.

Grace had known she would need someone to take care of Amy and Dan. A person who would keep them safe but was crazy enough to follow them on a hunt around the world. Nellie was the perfect candidate. Her family had been the guardians of a priceless Cahill treasure. She had a gift for foreign languages. And, as demonstrated by her elementary school transcript, she had no problem breaking rules. Grace knew that the Clue hunt wouldn't require Nellie to "liberate the class guinea pig," but it showed the right attitude.

Grace and William McIntyre sent endless opportunities Nellie's way to provide the training she'd need to help Amy and Dan on the hunt: languages, first aid, self-defense, and scuba diving. Looking back, Nellie realized that all these skills came into play, except for scuba diving. At least, so far . . .

MADRIGAL
HOT SPOTS

For almost five hundred years, the Madrigals have operated in complete secrecy, launching their crucial missions from a few carefully chosen bases around the world. They include:

CAHILL ISLAND, IRELAND
GENEVA, SWITZERLAND
THE HAGUE, THE NETHERLANDS
UNITED NATIONS HEADQUARTERS, USA

MADAGASCAR
ATTLEBORO, USA
EASTER ISLAND, CHILE

IRELAND

Even before he completed the master serum, Gideon Cahill had rivals desperate to steal his research, so he moved his family from mainland Ireland to a deserted island off the coast. As Gideon grew closer to unlocking the secrets of the 39 Clues, he became increasingly paranoid. No one else was allowed on the island except for Damien Vesper, a decision that would cost Gideon his life. In later years, the Madrigals used Gideon's obsession with secrecy to their advantage. They bribed cartographers to exclude the island from maps of the region, and within a few generations, the island was completely forgotten.

MADAGASCAR

When rumors surfaced that Grace had found a Clue in Egypt, the Ekaterina leadership sent a team of commandos to break into her Attleboro mansion. They didn't find it, but the incident was a wake-up call for Grace. The image of an armed soldier knocking down the door to two-year-old Hope's bedroom haunted her for the rest of her life. For her family's safety, Grace decided to build her own secret stronghold somewhere far away and bought a plot of land deep in the jungles of Madagascar. It became her Clue-hunting base and an ultrasecure storage space for her most

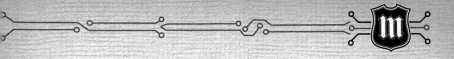

personal important possessions, from top secret documents to her beloved plane, *The Flying Lemur*.

UNITED NATIONS

Over the years, the Madrigal philosophy has expanded. In addition to reuniting the Cahill family, the Madrigals try to promote peace and cooperation among all people. They were responsible for founding the United Nations, an international organization that works to stop wars, provide aid, and uphold justice around the world. The UN headquarters in New York City functions as an unofficial Madrigal stronghold, as does the International Court of Justice in the Netherlands.

EASTER ISLAND

In the middle of the twentieth century, the Madrigals built a second stronghold on this Polynesian island famous for its enormous stone statues, or *moai*. Easter Island is one of the most isolated islands in the world—it's 2,180 miles off the coast of Chile—making it the ideal location for a secret base. The Madrigals built a fake moai to hide the entrance to their underground stronghold. The high-tech surveillance center allows them to track Cahill activity around the world.

LUCIANS

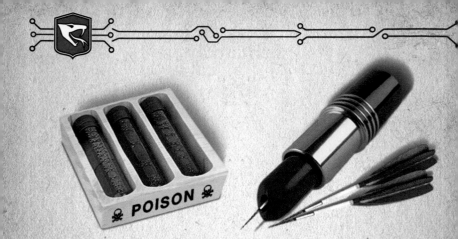

LUCIANS AT A GLANCE

Lucians are natural leaders. Throughout history, they've ruled countries, run global corporations, and led armies into battle. Whether managing political campaigns or businesses, their ruthlessness and talent for strategy always brings them out on top. While some Lucians succeed playing by the rules, this branch has a reputation for backstabbing and sabotage. They've even been behind some of history's most famous assassinations.

Lucian sneakiness also makes them excellent spies. Over the years, they've developed cutting-edge surveillance technology, as well as deadly weapons. The Lucians are particularly fond of hiding poison in commonplace items in order to catch their enemies by surprise.

LUCIAN CREST

The Lucian crest has changed over the years, but its central image has remained the same. The symbol for the Lucian branch has always been a double-headed snake. Like their favorite

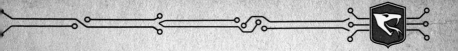

animal, Lucians value stealth and sneak attacks. Sometimes, victims don't even know they're a target until Lucian poison is seeping through their veins.

BRANCH LEADERS

Running the Lucian branch is one of the most dangerous jobs on earth. Lucians crave power and naturally want to occupy the top position. The leaders have to accept that the world's most highly trained spies and assassins could be hatching a plot to kill them at any moment.

The Lucians don't vote for their leaders; a Lucian election would end in a bloodbath. Instead, the branch leaders get to choose their successors—generally relatives or protégés. This system limits the number of leadership-related murders.

The current heads are Vikram and Isabel Kabra, married art dealers based out of London, although they have homes on nearly every continent. They conspire with top Lucians in the secret vault under their mansion and also oversee meetings at Lucian strongholds around the world. Or at least they did . . . until Isabel was arrested for murder.

STRONGHOLDS

Unlike other branches, which often hide their bases, the Lucians tend to place their strongholds in plain sight. They've always had access to fortresses, castles, armories, treasury vaults, and other secure buildings

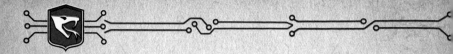

around the world where they can hold meetings, hide Clues, and interrogate enemies. The main Lucian strongholds in operation today include buildings in Paris, Moscow, and London.

LUCIAN INFLUENCE AROUND THE WORLD

The Lucians dominate politics and business in nearly every country on earth. They've produced the world's most powerful kings, queens, presidents, prime ministers, ambassadors, bankers, and entrepreneurs. Lucians *love* to show off their wealth, which, despite their spy training, makes them easy to spot in a crowd. Just look for the person wearing the diamond-encrusted gold watch, standing on the deck of a yacht, watching the maid feed the rare albino cat its lunch—$2,000-an-ounce caviar.

The Lucians' hunt for the 39 Clues has shaped history. They've founded nations, sparked revolutions, waged wars, and assassinated royalty in order to get closer to their goal. In 1914, the world was shocked when Archduke Ferdinand of Austria was shot in Serbia. Most people believe that the killer had political motives. But Cahill insiders know that the archduke was a Janus and the assassin was a Lucian desperate to find a Clue connected to the Austrian royal family. This event is considered to be one of the triggers of the First World War, one of the bloodiest conflicts of all time.

LUCIAN
FOUNDERS

Luke Cahill

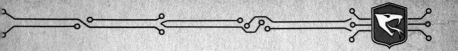

Natural-born leaders with unstoppable ambition, Lucians know how to inspire *and* how to manipulate. The Lucian founder Sidney George Reilly, known as the Ace of Spies, faked his own death, stole defense plans from the Japanese, and crashed a meeting of the German army high command. He was a real-life James Bond. The most famous—and infamous—Lucians include:

BENJAMIN FRANKLIN
CHING SHIH
GUSTAVE EIFFEL
SIDNEY GEORGE REILLY
ANASTASIA ROMANOV
WILLIAM STOUGHTON
NAPOLEON BONAPARTE
CATHERINE THE GREAT
THEODORE ROOSEVELT
ISAAC NEWTON
QUEEN VICTORIA
WINSTON CHURCHILL

GUSTAVE EIFFEL
12.15.1832–12.27.1923
ARCHITECT/ENGINEER

LUKE CAHILL (1484–?)

The eldest Cahill child and the founder of the Lucian branch, Luke was never content with his portion of the Clues. He dreamed of using his talents to create an empire—a kingdom in which people would be treated fairly. However, Luke wasn't naïve enough to think he could do it alone. He knew he needed all 39 Clues to accomplish his ambitious goals. But after his siblings falsely accused him of conspiring to kill their father, something changed. Luke became obsessed with revenge—more focused on destroying his siblings than realizing his own vision. He traveled to England, where he used his political gifts to become one of King Henry VIII's

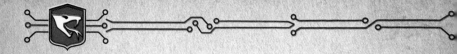

top advisers. Over the years, his anger toward his siblings festered. Court life taught Luke that anything is possible, especially if one is willing to use bribery, blackmail, and other forms of "persuasion." With the king's resources at his disposal, Luke began sending spies throughout Europe to look for his siblings, authorizing them to use "any means necessary" to find their Clues.

BENJAMIN FRANKLIN (1706–1790)

A founder of the United States, Benjamin Franklin was also world famous as a scientist and as an inventor. (He came up with bifocals, the lightning rod, and even the odometer.) However, few people know that he was also a top Lucian. In between his experiments with electricity and his work as ambassador to France, Franklin astonished his branch leadership by discovering all the Lucian Clues . . . and then hiding them from his branch. Franklin was a proud Lucian, but he was heartbroken to see how the hunt for the Clues brought out the worst in his fellow agents. He decided to bury the Clues rather than let other Lucians get their hands on them.

CHING SHIH (c. 1775–1844)

The feared pirate Ching Shih embodies Lucian ruthlessness. She was one of the most successful Clue hunters of her time, tracking leads all over east Asia. Ching Shih was infamous for punishing pirates who betrayed her—deserting cost you your

54

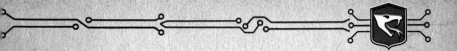

ears; thieves were beheaded. Despite her long list of crimes, she negotiated a deal with the Chinese government that allowed her to keep her stolen treasure and continue searching for Clues.

GUSTAVE EIFFEL (1832–1923)

Architecture is generally an Ekaterina profession. However, Gustave Eiffel combined design genius with a Lucian's cunning ambition. He built structures all over the world that became important Lucian bases. Eiffel's most famous works are the Statue of Liberty and the Eiffel Tower, but these monuments have a secret purpose—they were actually designed to hide Lucian Clues.

WILLIAM STOUGHTON (1631–1701)

Stoughton was a judge in the Salem witch trials—when innocent people in colonial America were accused of witchcraft and hanged for their "crimes." Stoughton was sent to New England to steal Clues from other branches. In order to eliminate his rivals, he and his fellow Lucians accused other Cahills of being witches. Their goal was to remove all Ekaterinas, Tomas, and Janus from New England and steal their Clues. Only twenty of the accused were executed, but the Salem witch trials showed just how far the Lucians were willing to go to stop their rivals.

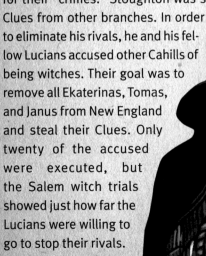

Founder Archives: Winston Churchill

Winston Churchill knew that a lot of people were jealous of his house, but he didn't feel too bad. They didn't have to sleep under the same roof as their dead relatives. Winston sat up and slowed his horse, Rob Roy, to a walk. Even from a distance, Blenheim Palace looked enormous with its soaring columns, expansive grounds, and private chapel that included a mausoleum. He shuddered slightly. Winston had lived at Blenheim his whole life, but eleven years weren't enough to get used to attending church services surrounded by his ancestors' tombs.

At least dead relatives can't criticize you, he thought. He had plenty of living relations to do that for him. He felt heat rise to his cheeks as he replayed the scene from that morning. He'd been so excited when his father, Lord Randolph, had summoned Winston to his study. His father was about to depart on a trip to South Africa, and Winston had spent the past few weeks campaigning to go with him. He knew other Lucian agents sometimes brought their older children with them on missions, and Winston was dying for the chance to prove himself.

What a waste, he thought bitterly as he urged his horse forward. When he'd walked into the study, his father had simply begun reading Winston's school report in a quiet, expressionless voice. After he'd finished, he'd shaken his head. "For centuries, this family has been devoted to two things." He'd raised his eyebrows at Winston.

"To country and to the clues," Winston had said quickly.

"Correct. And how do you ever expect to grow into a great leader, or a top Lucian agent, if you can hardly pass Geometry?"

Winston had just stared at the floor until his father had dismissed him. Yet now, after a two-mile gallop across the estate, his head was full of all the things he should have said.

If you could see what I've done with my cryptography tutor . . .
If you knew how many hours I've spent studying the globe . . .

If you knew how far I've come along with my Zulu . . .

But now it was too late. His father had already left for London. He might already have boarded the ship bound for South Africa. It could be years before Winston got another chance.

Out of the corner of his eye, Winston saw a flash of black. Too dark to be a deer. Rob's ears pricked up and he raised his head. Winston urged the horse forward, knowing that they'd make little noise on the soft, mossy ground.

"Lord Randolph is gone," Winston heard a man's voice say. He felt his heart speed up.

"Then I suppose it's time," said another. "Though it won't be easy climbing up on the roof in broad daylight."

"That's why the leadership gave us permission to use extreme measures."

Winston felt a surge of panic. His father had plenty of political rivals. Could they be assassins? He leaned forward to get a better look. The men were mounted on enormous horses and were dressed all in black except for the blue bear emblems on their lapels.

Winston gasped. Tomas. They must have sneaked onto the grounds. *There might be something connected to the clues in the palace.*

Without thinking, Winston spun Rob around, dug in his heels, and galloped off. He had no idea there was anything at Blenheim. His father had never even let a hint slip. But there was no time to worry about that now.

The Tomas had been on the edge of the road and would probably approach quietly. If Winston took the shortcut through the woods at a gallop, he could beat them to the palace by about ten minutes.

By the time they arrived, both he and Rob were panting. He swung his leg over the saddle and slid down, feeling the horse's sweat against his own damp shirt. He dropped the reins and ran inside, tearing up four flights of stairs to the corridor where there was a trapdoor to the top of the palace.

The sunlight was blinding as Winston stumbled onto the roof, gasping for breath. He shielded his eyes as he turned to look at the road. Two dark figures were moving toward the palace. They would reach the entrance in less than five minutes.

He scanned the roof, or at least as much as he could see of it. Every few yards, another tower shot up, blocking his view. It'd be impossible to cover more than a tenth of it before the riders reached the palace. He felt his stomach twist as the agent's words echoed in his head. *Extreme measures.* Winston knew the Cahills had done terrible things to each other on the hunt for the Clues. But he never expected anything to happen in his own home.

He took a breath, trying to stay calm even as his brain raced. How could anything be hidden here? There were no cracks. No loose stones. Nothing except—

Winston's eyes rested on the bust of the French king and Tomas agent Louis XIV. Blenheim Palace had been given to the first Duke of Marlborough, Winston's ancestor, as reward for winning an important battle against the French. In typical Lucian spirit, the Duke had ordered a bust of his rival to be placed on top of the palace, so the vanquished king could look down at his victor's accomplishments.

Winston dashed over to the bust and knelt down to examine it. His eyes scanned over the head. Nothing. He looked back at the road. The figures were growing larger and they seemed to have picked up speed—clouds of dust were billowing behind them. Winston turned back to the bust and began running his hands along the warm stone. He stopped as his fingers brushed against a carving of some sort. There were symbols etched into the back of the stone head. A code.

Winston felt a rush of excitement. He recognized the symbols; he had studied that cipher with his cryptography tutor. He scanned the message and, muttering to himself, began to crack the code.

"A dead Lucian duke is stronger than a live Tomas king." He inhaled sharply. There was something hidden in the family crypt.

The inside of the chapel was dark and cool. Without candles, the only illumination came from the late afternoon light shining faintly through the stained glass windows. His eye focused on the large sarcophagus against the wall. If he had understood the message correctly, the first Duke of Marlborough had ordered a Tomas Clue to be buried with him.

A scream made Winston turn to the window. A terrified kitchen maid stood on the lawn, pointing to something on the roof. He knew the Tomas agents must have found a way up.

Winston ran over to the tomb and began running his fingers along the life-sized sculpture of the duke resting on the marble slab. He tried not to think about what was inside. When he reached the feet, he stopped and crouched down. There was a tiny carving of a snake strangling a bear. Winston leaned in and spotted a faint crack around the sculpture's ankle. He grabbed the foot and pulled. It came off. The inside was hollow. Without stopping to think about how he was defacing his ancestor's tomb, Winston reached in and extracted a roll of parchment. He unrolled the crumbling document with shaky hands. Winston squinted as he tried to make out the faded letters. He recognized the words *serum* and *Zulu warriors*.

Grasping the parchment in his hand, Winston leaped to his feet and ran out of the chapel. He sprinted through the hallway and out the door, whistling to Rob Roy. In one swift move, he sprang into the saddle and took off at a gallop down the road. He glanced behind them and saw the men on the roof staring at him. He couldn't make out their expressions, but Winston could imagine what their faces would look like when they discovered they'd been outwitted by an eleven-year-old. Despite his racing heart and rapid breathing, Winston managed to smile. This had to count for more than Geometry. ✤

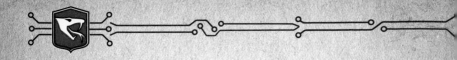

ANASTASIA ROMANOV (1901–1918?)

The Grand Duchess Anastasia of Russia was the youngest daughter of the last Russian tsar, Nicholas II. Anastasia's brother, Alexei, suffered from hemophilia, and their mother's desperate search for a cure led her to Grigori Rasputin, a man who claimed to be a healer. She had no idea that Rasputin was secretly a Tomas spy.

When the Russian revolution began, the other Cahills tried to encourage feelings of hatred toward the royal family. In 1917, Anastasia's father gave up the throne, and the family was placed under house arrest in Yekaterinburg, more than a thousand miles from their home in St. Petersburg. In 1918, the Romanovs were executed: the tsar, his wife, and their five children. Or, at least, that's what most people believe. For nearly a century, the Lucians have worked to hide the truth— Anastasia survived.

After she escaped, Anastasia assumed a fake identity and moved to a small town outside of Moscow, where she met Vladimir Radov, a Lucian agent. As an adult, Anastasia became a committed Clue hunter. Haunted by the memory of her family's murder, she was obsessed with the idea of ultimate power. Once she had it, she'd never have to worry about anyone harming her loved ones again.

NAPOLEON BONAPARTE
(1769–1821)

Napoleon Bonaparte was born in Corsica to inactive Lucians. As soon as he learned about the 39 Clues, Napoleon became obsessed with the hunt. He convinced his parents to let him attend military school close to the Lucian stronghold in Paris. After graduation he joined the French army and shot up through the ranks.

In a branch with the most competitive people in history, Napoleon became the most ambitious of them all. He soon gained control over the army and used it as a private Clue-hunting force.

When Napoleon invaded Egypt in 1798, he brought a team of scientists with him. In 1799, they found exactly what he was after—the Rosetta Stone, an ancient Egyptian artifact hiding a Clue. However, in 1801, British Ekaterinas attacked Napoleon's troops and seized the stone, placing it in the British Museum for safekeeping in 1802.

Despite these Clue-hunting mishaps, Napoleon was eventually named Emperor of France. The other branches grew so nervous about him that they formed a coalition army—the first in Cahill history. Led by a Tomas agent, the Duke of Wellington, they attacked Napoleon and defeated him at the battle of Waterloo.

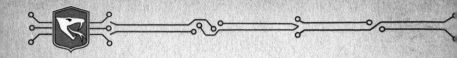

IRINA SPASKY (1964–2008)

At 16, Irina Spasky broke into her school in the middle of the night, disabling the alarm system with a paper clip. She opened a locked filing cabinet to access her class's official transcripts and lower the grades of the students who made fun of her eye twitch. A week later, she was recruited by the KGB and became their youngest agent ever.

When Irina turned 18, the KGB sent her undercover to Oxford University. She met Vikram Kabra and Isabel Vesper-Hollingsworth, who introduced Irina to their elite circle of friends. Then, during one of their secret parties, Isabel and Vikram took Irina aside and made a life-changing announcement — Irina was a member of the Lucian branch.

With her KGB training and her fierce intelligence, Irina quickly became a top agent. She tracked Clues to all corners of the world and became famous for her poison fingernails. Yet there was one person who saw Irina as something other than a terrifying Lucian. Her son, Nikolai, loved her more than anything in the world. When Isabel Kabra ordered Irina on a mission while Nikolai was ill, Irina tried to delay. However, Isabel refused to listen. Irina set off and returned days later, only to learn that Nikolai had died unexpectedly, without his mother nearby to hold his hand or hear his final words.

LUCIAN

AGENTS

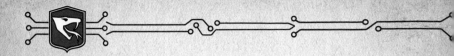

Lucians are supposed to wait until they've completed their agent training before they start hunting for Clues. However, the leadership often makes exceptions for particularly talented young agents. Today's top Lucian agents include:

ISABEL KABRA
VIKRAM KABRA
IAN KABRA
NATALIE KABRA
IRINA SPASKY
CHRISSY COLLINS
ANDRAS GERGELY
ALANA FLORES
BARACK OBAMA
NATALIYA RUSLANOVNA RADOVA
SPY MONKEYS
CLYDE SILVERMAN

ISABEL KABRA

Isabel Vesper-Hollingsworth was an inactive Lucian before she went to university and met Vikram Kabra, the son of the Lucian branch leader. She rose rapidly through the ranks, distinguishing herself as a ruthless interrogator. Without breaking a sweat, or even breaking a nail, Isabel could make the most hardened agents spill their secrets. After she married Vikram, she began working as an art dealer and became a fixture in the London social scene. Photographers couldn't get enough of the stunning, stylish Isabel. Everyone outside the Cahill family was shocked when they learned the truth—that beneath the designer clothes lies a killer.

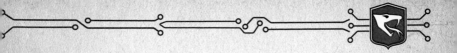

ALANA FLORES

Alana's cutthroat ambition and scheming mind make her a terrifying enemy. After conquering the world of competitive chess, Alana was fast-tracked by the Lucian leadership through agent training. She operates out of Hong Kong, working at a bank during the day and Clue hunting at night. Alana is one of the only Lucians who isn't terrified of Isabel, which makes her either incredibly brave or an "accident" waiting to happen.

NATALIYA RUSLANOVNA RADOVA

As the daughter of the Grand Duchess Anastasia and former Lucian leader Vladimir Radov, Nataliya Ruslanovna Radova is Lucian royalty. However, a blood disorder prevented her from going on Clue-hunting expeditions. Instead, Nataliya fulfilled her branch duties from inside the Moscow stronghold. Her gift for languages and code breaking made her the ideal mission leader. Yet despite her success, it became difficult for Nataliya to listen as her agents lied to allies and to watch as they slipped their rivals poison. At the urging of Grace Cahill, Nataliya began to think of ways to stop the Lucians from getting too powerful. That's why she chose to assist Amy and Dan, betraying her branch to serve as a Madrigal double agent.

CHRISSY COLLINS

Chrissy's parents are retired Lucian agents who chose to raise their children away from the Cahill world. However, Chrissy has always wanted to join the hunt. She began training on her own, practicing acrobatics, lock picking, computer programming, and code cracking. When she discovered that her hometown of Frankfort, Kentucky, was near a Lucian stronghold, she took action. At 17, she attempted to break into Fort Knox and nearly succeeded. Luckily, the Kabras intervened before Chrissy became the first cheerleader sent to federal prison.

The branch leadership knew that Chrissy had the potential to become a Clue-hunting legend, so they sent her to Paris for advanced agent training. She excelled at advanced cryptography but had trouble with poison mixing. Chrissy is dedicated to Lucian victory, but she doesn't like the idea of slipping arsenic in her rivals' drinks. Before she was arrested, Isabel Kabra had been working on a plan to cure Chrissy's "squeamishness." Luckily, Isabel ended up in jail before she had time to begin step one— forcing Chrissy to practice poisoning gerbils.

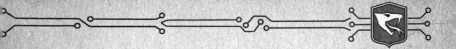

IAN KABRA

When Ian and Natalie returned to London after the Clue hunt, they assumed they'd have to live as fugitives. Their mother was in police custody, but they'd still have to answer to their father and the rest of the Lucian branch. No one would understand what had happened on the island. After five hundred years of Lucian scheming, plotting, and sacrifice, Ian and Natalie had let the final Clue slip through their fingers.

However, hours after Isabel was arrested, Vikram Kabra chartered a plane to Brazil to avoid questioning. The top Lucians in London also went into hiding before the police could associate them with Isabel's crimes.

With Isabel in prison and Vikram in hiding, there was no one to run the family's multimillion-pound art dealership. Ian stepped in and began meeting with high-profile clients around the world. Despite his young age, they were struck by his charm, and Ian soon discovered his specialty—convincing very rich old ladies to buy extremely ugly paintings that no one else wanted.

He's currently trying to get Jonah Wizard to take him on a tour of the Janus stronghold in Venice. He's not interested in stealing any Clues, but he's eager to visit the secret art gallery—there could be a Picasso small enough to hide in his jacket.

IAN KABRA

14
LUCIAN

LONDON, ENGLAND

AGENT UPDATE: Ian Kabra

It was the smiling that really drove him mad. Ian couldn't imagine what made everyone in Boston so cheerful. It wasn't the weather. The sky was a dreary gray, and as he glanced out the window, he saw people cocooned in hats and scarves, fighting their way against the wind. It certainly wasn't because they were all incredibly wealthy. The woman sitting at the next table was even wearing a faux fur jacket. Ian shuddered at the thought of artificial fibers rubbing against his professionally exfoliated skin. He could tolerate considerable hardship, but chafing was just too much to bear.

Yet everyone kept smiling at him. The portly, bald man who had checked them in. The bellboy who took their bags upstairs. The maid who came to their room after Natalie had called to complain that her pillowcases didn't match. And now, the waitress standing in front of them. She was beaming, as if Ian had just handed her a puppy with a Visa Black card in its mouth.

"Can I get you anything else?" she asked as she cleared their untouched plates. "It doesn't look like you enjoyed your breakfast very much!"

"Just the bill, please."

She smiled. "Are you going to do some sightseeing today? The first stop on the Freedom Trail is just around the corner. If you go ask Bob over there at the front desk, he can—"

"We have other plans," Ian interrupted.

"That's great! Anything fun?"

Natalie looked up at the waitress and gave her a fake smile. Except that on Natalie, it looked more demonic than cheerful. "Our mum's on trial for murder. Today's the verdict. But if it ends early, we'll be sure to pop by the Freedom Trail." The waitress's smile vanished.

Yet by the time they arrived in the courtroom, Ian found himself missing the excessive cheerfulness. No one at the Massachusetts Superior Court seemed to smile at all. For the first time since they'd arrived in Boston the night before, the real purpose of their trip sunk in. This wasn't one of their Christmas holidays when they'd take the jet to Boston so Isabel could go shopping on Newbury Street. He and Natalie were sitting on a hard wooden bench in a cold courtroom. And Mum wasn't off trying on clothes at Prada.

Everyone stood up as the judge walked in, his black robes billowing from the drafts. Two guards followed, escorting a tall woman in an orange jumpsuit. It was Isabel. The last time Ian and Natalie had seen her, she was being lifted into the Starlings' plane, unconscious. William McIntyre had made sure the police were waiting for her when they landed back in England.

Standing under the fluorescent lights, it was clear she wasn't wearing any makeup. Yet despite the bags under her eyes, she looked younger. Ian couldn't remember ever seeing his mother without lipstick. Her pale mouth made something in his stomach twitch. Like he was viewing something that was supposed to stay hidden.

He turned to whisper to Natalie, but she was staring straight ahead. Not at Isabel. Not at anyone. She wasn't moving, but Ian could see her jaw muscle tightening. It always happened when Natalie was trying not to cry. He took her hand and gave it a squeeze. She didn't react.

Ian couldn't imagine what Natalie was feeling. The last time she had been with her mother, Isabel had shot her in the foot. Yet, over the past few months, Ian kept catching Natalie in Isabel's room. He'd even found her asleep in their mother's closet, her head resting on a cashmere jumper. Natalie had claimed that she was simply sorting through Isabel's belongings, deciding what to keep and what to give to charity. But none of the clothes ever left the closet.

The judge banged his gavel. Ian felt Natalie flinch. The jurors filed in, taking their seats on the bench against the side wall. They all avoided eye contact with Isabel, but Ian could see her watching them, wrinkling her nose. He couldn't tell if she was sneering in anticipation of their decision or simply mocking their outfits.

"Has the jury reached a verdict?" the judge asked.

A woman in a blue pantsuit rose. "Yes, Your Honor."

"Proceed."

The juror cleared her throat. "In the matter of the Commonwealth of Massachusetts versus Isabel Kabra, we find the defendant guilty of murder in the first degree."

Although he tried to look away, Ian couldn't keep his eyes off his mother's face. It didn't move; her bored, snooty expression remained the same. He saw her lawyer lean over and whisper in her ear. She smiled slightly.

"Bailiff, remove the prisoner."

Ian watched as a guard handcuffed Isabel and began walking her down the aisle, toward the front door. For the first time in his life, Ian saw people look at his mother with something other than awe or fear. Everyone in the courtroom was staring at her in disgust.

As she passed Ian and Natalie, her eyes locked on to Ian's for a moment, and then she looked away.

A crowd of reporters had gathered outside of the courthouse. When Isabel came out, there was a flurry of camera flashes and eagar shouts as the guards tried to push through the press toward the armored prison van.

"Isabel, do you feel guilty?"

"Why'd you do it?"

"Where's your husband?"

"What's going to happen to the yacht?"

"Do you have any regrets about your children?"

Isabel frowned and faced the reporter who'd asked the last question. "I regret failing my children. I allowed them to grow up as weak-minded fools without the strength to make hard decisions." She paused and looked at Ian. "They'll never amount to anything," she said before turning back to the press. Although her hands were cuffed, she managed to toss her long hair over her shoulder with a graceful flip of her head. "*They'll* never be in the papers."

Let her have her last moment in the spotlight, Ian thought as he led Natalie down the courthouse steps. After a life devoted to charming guests at cocktail parties and terrorizing the world's top spies at Lucian meetings, she was going to spend the rest of her days in federal prison. Soon, her name would fade from everyone's memory. It would disappear from newspapers, from lists of benefactors, from social registers. The woman who had been so desperate to take over the world would be erased. There was no more Isabel Kabra. Only prisoner number 44850. ✤

RDAOXONMYSEDSAZY

IGNORE THE ODD ONES

NATALIE KABRA

AGE 11
BRANCH LUCIAN
HOMETOWN:
LONDON, ENGLAND

MADRIGAL SURVEILLANCE NETWORK

--START--

[sound of a bell ringing followed by locker doors slamming]

SOPHIE: Hey. You came back.

NATALIE: [overly cheery] Oh, yes. We were yachting in the Caribbean. It was so lovely. [pause]

SOPHIE: I know what happened to your mother. . . . I'm sorry.

NATALIE: [startled] What? Are you talking about the—I mean, how would you know about any of that?

SOPHIE: If you had spent less time applying lip gloss, you might have noticed that I've been spying on you for the Janus.

NATALIE: You're a Cahill? I suppose I should've known. Only a Janus would wear such ridiculous outfits. [pause] So . . . everyone knows, then? What happened in Ireland?

SOPHIE: Sort of. I think. Cora sent a strange e-mail around. I heard my parents talking about it. Everyone's furious at Jonah. They feel like five hundred years of work all went to waste.

NATALIE: [softly] The Lucians aren't that, um, happy, either.

SOPHIE: I think you did the right thing.

NATALIE: Thanks. [pause] You know, that skirt you're wearing isn't completely dreadful.

SOPHIE: [laughs] I like your dress.

NATALIE: Thanks. [pause] This is the first time I've chosen a back-to-school outfit without my mum. I suppose I have to get used to it.

SOPHIE: Picking your own clothes?

NATALIE: Making my own decisions.

[rest of conversation obscured by bell and hallway noise]

--END--

CLASSIFIED

LUCIAN
TRICKS & TOOLS

Lucians are experts at secrecy, sabotage, and, above all, lying. When equipped with the advanced spy gear they've been developing for centuries, the Lucians are nearly unstoppable Clue hunters. Their go-to tricks and tools include:

POISON-DELIVERY MECHANISMS
POISON RINGS
POISON FINGERNAILS
POISON DARTS
POISON CUFF LINKS
POISON TEDDY BEARS
POISON UMBRELLAS

WEAPONS
DAGGERS
RETRACTABLE KNIVES
WALKING-STICK SWORDS
BULLET PENS

TRANSPORTATION
THE SHARK
BULLETPROOF LIMOUSINES
ADVANCED FIGHTER JETS
SPEED YACHTS (WITH HELIPADS)

COMMUNICATION
CODES
SURVEILLANCE BUGS
UNTRACEABLE CELL PHONES
POLYGRAPHS

POISON

Lucians have been using poison for centuries; it's the perfect tool for sneak attacks and silent assassinations. Over the years, the Lucians have developed special poisons that are almost impossible to detect. They like to do their dirty work as quickly and quietly as possible.

POISON RINGS

Poison rings have always been a favorite among royal Lucians, or those serving as advisers to kings and queens. One could attend a feast or a ball while carrying a lethal dose of poison—a common practice among Lucians. With their tiny injector needles, poison rings only work when agents can get close to their victims. That's what makes the Lucians so dangerous—they can smile at you one moment and then jab you with a poison ring before you even have a chance to smile back.

POISON FINGERNAILS

As ornate rings fell out of fashion, it became necessary to hide poison in even sneakier ways. One alternative was cunning poison fingernails—tiny needles that can be hidden under the nail and then extended with a flick of the finger. The other branches particularly fear this Lucian invention, as they're nearly impossible to detect and can make the simplest of acts—like a handshake—turn deadly.

TRANSPORTATION
The Shark

While the Ekaterina branch might produce the best engineers, the Lucians have always been on the cutting edge of surveillance and transportation technology. The Shark, a revolutionary heli-copter hidden at the Lucian stronghold in Moscow, can fly at up to three hundred miles per hour and is undetectable by most radar.

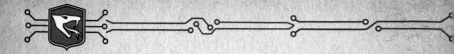

Bulletproof Limousines

These extremely expensive cars are generally associated with presidents, prime ministers, and other people at high risk for assassination. The most recent line of Lucian-designed limos are bulletproof, bombproof, and fireproof. The windows are equipped with hidden retina scanners, so passengers can tell who is trying to sneak a peek through the tinted glass.

COMMUNICATION

Codes

The Lucians excel at crafting and cracking codes. Since Lucian strategy depends on secrecy, it's essential that they have secure methods of sending information. Their favorites include:

AIRPORT DEPARTURE BOARD CODES
ANAGRAMS
MIRROR WRITING
SUBSTITUTION CODES
PICTOGRAMS
PIG PEN CODES
NAIL POLISH CODES
MOVIE POSTER CODES
iPOD CODES

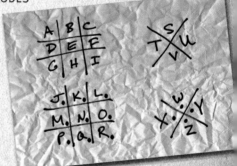

Polygraphs/Body Language Analysis

The Lucians are expert liars, which also makes them expert lie detectors. They also study body language, which makes it nearly impossible to lie to a Lucian. One nose twitch or eyebrow movement, and a trained Lucian will know exactly what you're thinking—and even where you hid your Clue.

LUCIAN
HOT SPOTS

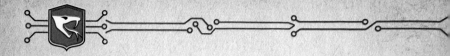

Most non-Cahills wouldn't think anything strange if they walked into a Lucian stronghold. However, more observant visitors could notice images of snakes carved in unexpected places. They might strain their ears and wonder if those are really screams they're hearing in the distance. They might even ask themselves why some people who go in, never come out. Lucian-dominated regions and sites include:

THE TOWER OF LONDON

BLETCHLEY PARK, UK

PASSY, FRANCE

PALACE OF VERSAILLES, FRANCE

THE PARIS CATACOMBS, FRANCE

THE MOSCOW KREMLIN, RUSSIA

SALEM, USA

HUNGARIAN PARLIAMENT

YEKATERINBURG, RUSSIA

EIFFEL TOWER, FRANCE

AREA 51, USA

FORT KNOX, USA

THE KABRA MANSION, UK

WALL STREET, USA

KABRA MANSION

The most important Lucian leadership meetings are currently held in the Kabra mansion in London. All visitors undergo a full body scan before entering the high-security meeting room in a titanium vault underneath the house. The entrance is protected by retina scans and voice-activated laser shields.

THE MOSCOW KREMLIN

For centuries, the Moscow Kremlin, the center of the Russian government, was one of the most secure complexes in the world. It was closed to tourists until 1955 and, even today, there are areas that you would not want to wander into accidentally. The Lucians built a top secret stronghold under the State Kremlin Palace. When Lucians in Russia want to make someone disappear,

they bring their victim to the prison on the bottom level. With its soundproof walls and single-prisoner cells, it's been known to drive even the toughest Cahills mad.

WALL STREET

Lucians don't always use their cunning to take over countries. During the last century, Lucians became incredibly powerful on Wall Street—the financial heart of the United States. There is even a secret Lucian meeting room hidden inside the New York Stock Exchange. Often, before the market opens, Lucian stockbrokers teleconference with their fellow branch members in different parts of the world to come up with a strategy for the day—a plan that will earn billions of dollars for Lucians around the globe.

THE TOWER OF LONDON

Begun in 1078, the Tower of London has served as a palace, a fortress, a royal zoo, and as a prison for aristocratic enemies of the state. Many people are familiar with the famous prisoners executed within its walls, but few know that most were rival Cahills the Lucians wanted to eliminate. In addition to killing their enemies, the Lucians also used the Tower of London for top secret meetings. The fortress's thick stone walls ensured that no one would overhear the Lucians' diabolical plans.

EKATERINAS

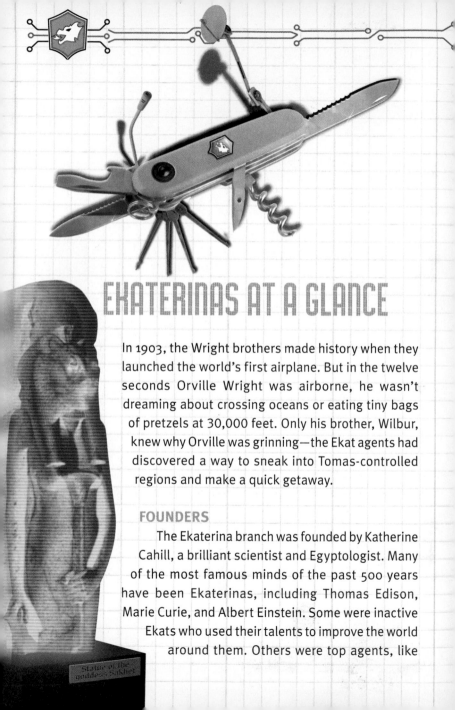

EKATERINAS AT A GLANCE

In 1903, the Wright brothers made history when they launched the world's first airplane. But in the twelve seconds Orville Wright was airborne, he wasn't dreaming about crossing oceans or eating tiny bags of pretzels at 30,000 feet. Only his brother, Wilbur, knew why Orville was grinning—the Ekat agents had discovered a way to sneak into Tomas-controlled regions and make a quick getaway.

FOUNDERS

The Ekaterina branch was founded by Katherine Cahill, a brilliant scientist and Egyptologist. Many of the most famous minds of the past 500 years have been Ekaterinas, including Thomas Edison, Marie Curie, and Albert Einstein. Some were inactive Ekats who used their talents to improve the world around them. Others were top agents, like

Statue of the goddess Sakhet

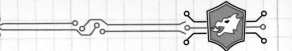

the Wright brothers, whose inventions were created for the Clue hunt.

BRANCH LEADERS

Ekaterina leadership is generally passed down within families. The last official branch head was Korean businessman Bae Oh, but he was recently arrested for a decades-old crime—the murder of Gordon Oh, his twin brother. According to Ekat tradition, Gordon's son, Alistair, should take over as branch leader. However, there are rumors that Alistair betrayed the Ekats by sharing his Clues with the other branches. The investigation is ongoing.

GORDON OH
1923 – 1948
EKATERINA LEADER

"GREAT SPIRITS
HAVE ALWAYS
ENCOUNTERED
VIOLENT OPPOSITION
FROM MEDIOCRE
MINDS."
—ALBERT EINSTEIN

STRONGHOLDS

The Ekat Clue hunt strategy has always been to develop cutting-edge technology, so most of their strongholds contain state-of-the-art laboratories. Their main stronghold is concealed within a luxury hotel in Cairo. It boasts one of the most advanced security systems in the world, with lasers, DNA scanners, and voice recognition devices. There are also Ekaterina bases in the Bermuda Triangle, at CERN on the border of France and Switzerland, and in the British Museum.

STRATEGY

The Ekaterinas have invented the best spy cameras and hacking devices, which means they always know what the other branches

are up to. This information has allowed the Ekaterinas to operate in quieter and sneakier ways than their Cahill rivals. However, the Ekats are still supremely dangerous. They become so focused on science that they can forget about the consequences of their work.

In addition to life-saving inventions, like antibiotics, they've created some of the most deadly weapons in the world—including the atomic bomb.

EKATERINA CREST

The symbol of the Ekaterina branch is the dragon. A mythological creature that appears in countless forms, the dragon represents the Ekats' creativity, inventiveness, and intelligence, but also their willingness to destroy anything that stands in their way.

EKATERINA
FOUNDERS

Katherine Cahill

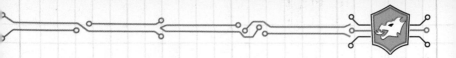

From John Flamsteed, the first royal astronomer and rival of Isaac Newton, to Albert Einstein, brilliant Ekaterinas have revolutionized the Clue hunt . . . and the way we think about the world. Ekat founders include:

ANNE CAHILL	HOWARD CARTER
THOMAS EDISON	T. E. LAWRENCE
NIKOLA TESLA	ORVILLE WRIGHT
DR. BERNHARD VON GUDDEN	WILBUR WRIGHT
ROBERT HENDERSON CAHILL	GORDON OH
SIR JOHN FLAMSTEED	ABRAHAM LINCOLN
MARIE CURIE	ALBERT EINSTEIN

KATHERINE CAHILL (1492–?)

The Ekaterina founder was the second child of Gideon and Olivia Cahill. Like her father, Katherine grew up fascinated by science. After she left Ireland, she became one of the world's first Egyptologists. She also learned to read ancient hieroglyphics three hundred years before the "first" official translators were even born. However, before she left for Egypt, Katherine made a decision that would shape the course of history. Angry with her favorite brother, Thomas, she stole one of his Clues and departed for faraway lands. As a result, the Ekaterinas and Tomas have been particularly bitter rivals for the past 500 years.

THOMAS EDISON (1847–1931)

Even before he learned about the Cahill family, Thomas Edison demonstrated all the qualities of a true Ekat. As a boy, he had a job selling candy and newspapers on trains. When business was slow, he'd conduct scientific experiments in a makeshift lab in the back of a car. This system worked well . . . until Edison caused a

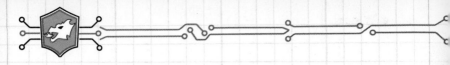

small explosion.

Despite this mishap, Edison became one of the most famous inventors of all time—he even came up with the lightbulb. Edison was also a devoted Ekat. After he discovered that one of Katherine's lost Clues was related to electricity, he began researching it furiously. However, Edison and his assistant, Ekat agent Nikola Tesla, disagreed about the best method to deliver electricity, and their feud became one of the most famous rivalries in the history of science.

T. E. LAWRENCE (1888–1935)

Thomas Edward Lawrence, known as Lawrence of Arabia, was an archaeologist and an officer in the British army. As a young man, he spent time in Egypt, excavating ancient sites. He learned that an Ekat Clue was connected to the Rosetta Stone, and tracked down a book about the artifact that contained a crucial hint. After the outbreak of World War I, he traveled to the Middle East and began working as a spy for the British. While he survived the war, the Lucians learned that Lawrence was guarding the book that held the key to the Ekat Clue. They arranged for him to be killed in a motorcycle "accident" in 1935.

ALEXANDER HAMILTON (1755–1804)

When the Madrigals first came to the American colonies, they

imagined a peaceful land free from the violence the Clue hunt had unleashed in other parts of the world. However, their dream was short-lived. By the time John Adams became president, Cahill blood had already been shed in the newborn country, and tensions were only heating up. Ekat Alexander Hamilton, the first secretary of the treasury, became obsessed with eliminating his Cahill rivals, particularly the Lucian vice president, Aaron Burr. Hamilton believed that he deserved to be vice president and, after the election, he continued to speak ill of Burr. With his honor at stake, Burr challenged Hamilton to a duel. Although most duels in that era ended with the participants shooting at the ground, Hamilton and Burr took aim at each other. Hamilton was mortally wounded and died the following day. This tragedy was the Madrigals' worst nightmare. It ensured that the future of the United States would be forever linked to the destructive power of the Clues.

GORDON OH (1923–1948)

Gordon Oh and his twin brother, Bae, were born to elite Ekat agents, and it was always accepted that one of the boys would run the branch. From childhood, Gordon was the obvious choice. However, he never had the chance to see his plans through. While Bae neglected his agent duties, he resented Gordon's success. In 1948, when Gordon's son, Alistair, was only four years old, Bae arranged for Gordon to be killed on a trip to New York. As he lay on the street, bleeding from his fatal wounds, Gordon managed to whisper a few words to his wife before he slipped out of consciousness—"Keep Alistair safe."

Founder Archives: Katherine Cahill

Katherine sat up with a jolt, woken by the pounding of her own heartbeat. She turned to the window and scanned the dark sky until she spotted the familiar shape. The starry plow was close to the horizon. It was about an hour before dawn. If she was really going to do it, she had to go now.

She wrapped her cloak around her shoulders, even though the Portuguese night was balmy. The less she had to carry, the better. Her equipment alone nearly filled her traveling bag. As she swung it over her shoulder, she could feel the brass telescope press against her back and the heavy scales dig into her hip.

She paused as she passed Thomas and his wife Louisa's room. His telltale snores were rattling the door. If Katherine went through with her plan, she'd never see Thomas again. She'd be severing the last tie to her family. For a moment, she was overcome by swirling memories. Sneaking out of the house to go star watching with Thomas. Dreaming about the adventures they'd have when they finally set sail from Ireland.

But the scientist in her won out. A surgeon would never hesitate to remove a rotten limb, no matter how loyally it had served the patient in the past.

It was time to make the first cut.

The study was locked, as always. For extra security, Katherine had designed a door that required two keys to open. Trying to suppress the twinge of guilt in her stomach, Katherine pulled two keys from her bag. She had slipped Thomas's out of his pocket at supper the night before.

The wooden trunk in the corner was also locked. Katherine and Thomas hadn't wanted to take any chances. It was only a matter of time before Luke's spies tracked them down.

A layer of dust covered the top of the trunk. It hadn't been opened since Katherine and Thomas moved to Portugal. They had planned on staying a few weeks. After Thomas met Louisa, he had begged Katherine for a little extra time. That had been three years ago.

Katherine had waited long enough. Luke was gaining power in England as the king's adviser. They had to take their Clues somewhere far, far away. China. Egypt. The New World. Any of the distant lands they had dreamed about. That's why they'd left Ireland. They abandoned their grieving mother, who, although she never stopped smiling, reminded Katherine of a flower that continued to bloom while it was dying. They had to keep their Clues safe, out of Luke's hands.

Or else, Katherine thought, *we broke our mother's heart for nothing.*

She unlocked the trunk, coughing as a cloud of dust engulfed her face. She wiped her eyes and peered in. She gasped. At first, she thought she must be mistaken, but then she looked again. It was true. There were only gold pouches inside. Or . . . she stuck her head in closer. Seven gold pouches and one single blue pouch with a bear symbol embroidered on it. Thomas had taken his Clues.

Her heart sank as she spotted the piece of folded parchment. With shaking fingers, she picked it up and unfolded it.

Dearest Sister,
Please forgive me. I have seen the look of restlessness on your face and feared that you might do something rash. Whatever you have planned, I beg you to reconsider. Together, we are strong. Alone, I fear we shall fall prey to the darkness that dwells within all of our family. I trust you will make the right decision in the end. I have left one of my Clues here to prove my faith—my belief that you would never betray me.
—Thomas

Katherine clapped her hand over her mouth to stop herself from screaming. Before they'd left Ireland, she and Thomas had decided to keep their Clues together until they found permanent hiding places for them. If Luke's spies attacked, they'd need to grab the Clues and go—there would be no time to go hunting through the house. However, they'd vowed never to look inside the others' pouches. But Thomas *hadn't* trusted her. He had broken his promise and taken his Clues! The mix of guilt and anxiety that had been bubbling in her stomach hardened into cold fury.

A sound from upstairs made Katherine jump. The footsteps were heavy. It was Thomas. She could hear the floorboards creaking under his weight. Without time to think, Katherine reached into the trunk and grabbed all the pouches—the seven gold ones, and the lone Clue Thomas had left behind.

Katherine reached the harbor just as the ship was raising its anchor. The gangplank had already been removed. She flung her bag on the deck and then leaped from the dock, grabbing on to a rope to keep herself from falling backward into the water. She collapsed on the deck. Her heart was beating so fast, she felt like her chest was going to explode. A group of sailors stared at her curiously, but she didn't mind. She had spoken with the captain the previous day and had paid for her passage to Egypt.

Once her pulse slowed down, Katherine rose to her feet, grabbing on to the railing for support. She was still slightly woozy from her sprint. She shook her head, willing the world to come back into focus. Katherine looked up as the ship started to drift away from the harbor. The sun had risen, and the fishermen were setting up their stalls. She could hear the drone of the market. Shouts of greeting. The grunts of the men as they hauled their catch up from their boats. The customers haggling good-naturedly for a low price.

Suddenly, another sound pierced through the buzz of the crowd—halfway between a clap of thunder and the howl of a wounded beast. Katherine watched in horror as Thomas crashed through a line of wooden carts, sending mounds of fish flying. He was charging at full speed down the dock. Even from the deck of the ship, Katherine could see that his face was red with rage.

"KATHERINE!" he roared. "Give it to me!"

She took a step back from the railing.

He was approaching at an impossible speed, his massive legs propelling him toward the ship.

"You can't do this!" he bellowed. "We made a promise!"

Katherine felt her face flush. She took a step forward. "A promise *you* broke when you kept us rotting here for three years, waiting for Luke like sitting ducks," she screamed. "You've forsaken your duty, Thomas. But you won't make me forsake mine."

He was a few yards away from the edge of the dock and showed no signs of slowing down. Everyone on the shore had turned to watch. The sailors had gathered on the deck as well. They stared in awe as Thomas took a flying leap, arcing through the air over the enormous gap between the ship and the edge of the dock.

There was a thud as his body connected with the side of the ship, one hand grasping on to a rope that was dangling off the side.

The boat was picking up speed as its sails unfurled. Even with his incredible strength, Thomas struggled to hold on.

"Give it to me now," he shouted to be heard over the wind. "Or you'll never forgive yourself."

"Is that man supposed to be joining you?" the captain asked, stepping forward.

She peered over the rail. Thomas's face was twisted in pain and fury. She watched his enormous muscles ripple from the effort of holding on.

"No."

The captain strode toward the edge, removing his sword from its sheath. With one swift movement, he cut the rope from which Thomas was hanging. Katherine watched as her brother dropped away. His eyes locked with hers as he fell fifty feet into the churning water below. ✤

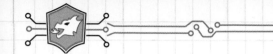

NIKOLA TESLA (1856–1943)

Tesla was a Serbian inventor known for his revolutionary work with electrical engineering and for his reputation as a mad scientist. He'd invite guests into his lab to make small talk while thousands of deadly volts of electricity crackled above their heads. He was obsessed with the number three and pigeons, and had an extremely keen sense of smell. He also had a bitter rivalry with fellow Ekat Thomas Edison.

While the branch leadership wanted their two most talented agents to work together, Edison and Tesla had a heated argument that sparked one of the most famous feuds in the history of science. Tesla continued his research on his own, even after the Madrigals deemed him too dangerous and destroyed his lab.

Tesla's wild experiments paid off. He discovered the Clue and, before his death, sent it to his family home in Croatia for safekeeping. It remained untouched for decades until Janus director Leslie D. Mill began filming a movie about Tesla, which inspired agents from all branches to track down the Clue.

Smiljan, Croatia, became a hotbed of Cahill activity, though only top Clue hunters figured out how to get past Tesla's defenses and find the mad scientist's Clue.

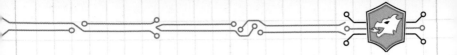

MARIE CURIE (1867–1934)

Marie Curie was a scientist who made groundbreaking discoveries in the field of radiation. She and her husband, Pierre, won the Nobel Prize in Physics in 1903, and Marie won the prize for Chemistry in 1911. However, only the Cahills know that the Curies' research was part of an attempt to discover a long-lost Clue.

Marie and Pierre understood it was only a matter of time before the other branches attacked. They took care to keep their laboratory locked and all crucial documents hidden. However, there were dangers neither scientist could anticipate. In 1906, Pierre was killed after being struck by a horse-drawn wagon.

Accounts of the incident varied. Some witnesses claimed that he simply slipped and fell in front of the wagon. Others claimed that the driver hit Pierre on purpose. The Lucians made sure those people disappeared quickly.

Although heartbroken, Marie continued with her work. In addition to her contributions to modern science, she distinguished herself by identifying the Clue, which was then sent to the Ekats' Bermuda Triangle stronghold for safekeeping. Tragically, Marie's success came at a high price. She spent the last years of her life slowly dying from radiation poisoning. To this day, her possessions are so radioactive, they must be kept in lead-lined boxes.

HOWARD CARTER (1874–1939)

Howard Carter was an archaeologist and Egyptologist famous for discovering the tomb of Tutankhamun, also known as King Tut. Like his ancestor Katherine Cahill, Carter was fascinated by the ancient Egyptians, but he had a secret reason for exploring ancient tombs. He believed that Katherine had hidden a Clue somewhere in Egypt, and that she had left hints inside four different statues of the goddess Sakhet.

Carter was so desperate to find the statues that he risked the legendary "curse of the pharaohs," the punishment for disturbing the tomb of an Egyptian king. Although most of the members of the expedition were skeptical of the myth, a number of people on Carter's team died shortly after the tomb was opened. Carter didn't believe in the curse, yet he recorded a number of strange events. A messenger sent to Carter's house found a cobra—the symbol of the Egyptian monarchy—resting in a birdcage. And once Carter started excavating the tomb, he began seeing jackals—the symbol of the guardian of the dead. Carter lived for another sixteen years, but he never found the last Sakhet statue; it was as if he was cursed to search forever.

EKATERINA
AGENTS

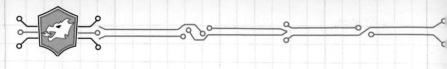

The Ekaterinas aren't really the mad scientists the other branches imagine. They might be visionary thinkers and world-class inventors, but many Ekat agents are also savvy Clue hunters who use their skills both in the lab and on the hunt. Current active Ekat agents possess a range of talents, from eleven-year-old treehouse engineer Devin Cooper to the legendary Apple founder Steve Jobs. They include:

ALISTAIR OH
BAE OH
LILYA CHERNOVA
VLADIMIR CHERNOV
VERA CHERNOVA
SINEAD STARLING

NED STARLING
TED STARLING
DEVIN COOPER
YASMEEN BADAWI
TEODORA KOSARA
VICTOR WOOD

LILYA CHERNOVA

Lilya Chernova is the daughter of two high-ranking Russian Ekats. Her Ekaterina roots are clear in her academic accomplishments— she's the best math student in her school's history. However, her real passion is for fashion. Some people call Lilya's outfits strange (Natalie Kabra calls them "vomit-inducing"), but she knows her critics simply lack imagination. After all, it takes a special person to wear a green sequined dress and magenta cowboy boots to a math competition.

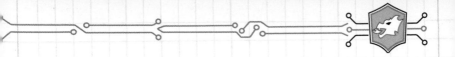

YASMEEN BADAWI

Twenty-year-old Yasmeen is a robotics engineer from the Cairo suburbs. After her mother was killed by the Lucians, Yasmeen spent much of her childhood at the Ekat headquarters taking classes, learning about the branch history, and dreaming about becoming a top agent, just like her mother. She distinguished herself as a rising star in the branch after she won a robotics contest and was asked to create a new security system for the Cairo stronghold. The hunt for the 39 Clues is particularly important to Yasmeen, as she considers her fellow Ekat agents to be her real family and will do whatever it takes to prove her loyalty.

THE STARLING TRIPLETS

Ned, Ted, and Sinead Starling spent their whole lives preparing for the Clue hunt. Even after an explosion at the Franklin Institute left the Starlings gravely injured, they refused to quit and managed to catch up with their competition. After the hunt, the triplets started college. Ted's seeing-eye dog, Flamsteed, became the most popular dorm resident after Sinead trained him to announce the dinner menu. Using his supercharged sense of smell, Flamsteed barks once for pizza, twice for hamburgers, and three times for mystery meat.

VICTOR WOOD

Chemistry student Victor Wood broke Ekat protocol when he used his university's lab to conduct top secret

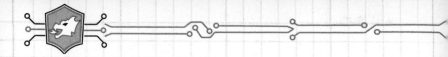

research on the Clues. However, rather than punish the ambitious young scientist, Bae selected him as his newest assistant. Now, Wood splits his time between his studies in London and his duties at the Cairo stronghold, where he spends a great deal of time in the ultrasecure lab. Unlike his relationship with his nephew, Alistair, Bae sees nothing but promise in Victor and believes he's the future of the Ekaterina branch.

TEODORA KOSARA

Growing up in Bulgaria, Teodora didn't have access to the same resources as young agents in real Ekat hot spots around the world. However, that didn't stop her from devoting herself to the Clue hunt, using every opportunity to conduct research and follow leads. While on a class trip to London, she even sneaked off to explore the Tower of London, a known Lucian stronghold. Teodora is obsessed with finding the 39 Clues, but her allegiance to the Ekaterinas is questionable. She has ties to the Vespers—the only other group in the world that knows about the Clues.

November, Echo,
Lima, Lima, India,
Echo, India,
Sierra, Alpha,
Tango, Alpha,
Romeo, Golf, Echo,
Tango

AGENT UPDATE: Alistair Oh

After saving the world, Dan deserved all the candy he could eat. At least, that's what he said as he plopped down into the seat across from Alistair, letting an armload of snacks fall into his lap.

They were in the Dublin airport. Mr. McIntyre had bought Amy, Dan, and Nellie tickets to Boston. Alistair was catching a flight to London and then was flying on to Seoul.

"Flight 2039 to Boston is now boarding at gate 14A," a voice announced over the PA system.

Nellie sighed. "I love Irish accents." She paused. "And Australian accents. And English accents." A dreamy look came over her face. "Theo had an *awesome* accent."

Dan snorted. "Yeah, there was just that one tiny problem. He turned out to be a two-timing, backstabbing thief."

Nellie rolled her eyes. "Whatevs. Everyone we met wanted to steal something from you."

"Or just kill us," Amy added softly. She hadn't spoken much since they'd left the island that morning. Alistair frowned. A fourteen-year-old shouldn't look that weary.

There had been so many close calls on the hunt. The explosion in Philadelphia. The fire in Indonesia. The events in the airplane hangar with Isabel. Alistair wasn't sure Amy and Dan even realized how many times they'd almost lost their lives. How near he'd come to breaking his promise to Hope.

Dan ripped open a Yorkie bar and took a huge bite. Amy stared at him warily. "You know the flight's only six hours, right? That looks like six *weeks*' worth of candy."

"I haf to shtock up," he said, spraying candy on her as he spoke.

"*Ewww!*" Amy squealed, trying to scrape the wet chocolate

flecks off her skin. "There's no way they're going to let you back in the country. You're a walking biohazard." Alistair sighed. He was going to miss the children.

As Nellie sorted their boarding passes, Amy and Dan stood to say good-bye. Amy gave him a brief hug. Dan, a longer one. Alistair held him tight, despite knowing there was a good chance he'd leave with chocolate on his suit.

As they walked away, he wondered when he'd get to see them again. Did one day of selflessness make up for six weeks of betrayal? Or, worse, for the lifetime they'd have to spend without their parents? All because Alistair had been too afraid to cross Isabel. Too afraid to challenge his uncle.

He stood up. Maybe it wasn't too late. He walked over to the ticket counter and switched his reservation from Seoul to Cairo.

Seven hours later, Alistair was standing in the lobby of Cairo's Hotel Excelsior. Everything felt surprisingly similar. The fountain trickled serenely in the corner. The smell of violets wafted from the bouquet on the concierge's desk. After all that had happened in Ireland, it was strange to find the hotel unchanged. As if the past few days had all been a dream.

He glanced at his watch. He had five minutes to get his uncle outside, or the plan might not work. But before Alistair had time to worry, the elevator pinged open and Bae emerged, flanked by two large men in dark suits. He'd taken the bait.

Bae walked forward until he was so close that Alistair could see his own reflection in his uncle's furious eyes.

"Is it true?" Bae shouted. His breath streamed across Alistair's face.

When Alistair didn't respond, Bae turned and nodded to the suited men. They strode forward and grabbed Alistair by the arms, pinning him against the hotel wall.

"I will not ask you again. Are the rumors true?" Bae's voice rose alarmingly, just like it had all those times he'd told Alistair that his report card was an embarrassment. That his last Clue-hunting mission was a dismal failure. Or that his father would've been ashamed of him . . .

Alistair felt himself being hoisted off the ground, so his legs were dangling in the air.

"You'll believe whatever you want to believe, uncle." The men tightened their grip, and one of them placed his enormous hands around Alistair's neck. He felt a palm press against his windpipe.

Bae leaned in closer. "What does that mean?" Alistair felt flecks of spit land on his eyelids. He tried to speak, but his words came out as ragged gasps. With a nod from Bae, the men released Alistair, letting him fall to the ground. He rolled onto his back and stared into the bright fluorescent lights.

"You . . . can . . . convince . . ." Alistair wheezed, each word scraping against his throat like a knife. ". . . yourself of anything. That you deserved to be branch head. That my father deserved to die."

Bae walked toward him. "You've always tried to blame me for your failures." His voice quivered with rage. "But I tried. It was you who never lived up to your potential."

Alistair rose to his feet and took a wobbly step. He had to get to the door.

"It was you who turned your back on me," Bae roared, watching Alistair shuffle forward. "You betrayed your branch. You're worse than a failure. You're a traitor."

The door was just a few yards away. He was almost there.

"I'm not going to let your weakness sabotage us again," Bae yelled as his cane came crashing down over Alistair's head.

Alistair collapsed on the floor. The cane struck again, sending a wave of agony through his body. He groaned as he stretched his arm forward. *I'm so close.*

Despite the pain in his side, he reached up and opened the door, groaning from the effort. With a grunt, he pulled himself into the sunlight. He heard Bae laugh bitterly. "You think you can crawl away? Another brilliant plan. I'm not—" He stopped short as he surveyed the scene in front him. The driveway was full of Hummers emblazoned with the United Nations symbol.

A man in fatigues stepped forward. "Bae Oh, you are under arrest for the murder of Gordon Oh, for the trafficking of illegal weapons, for the transport of hazardous materials"—he looked down at Alistair—"and for assault and battery."

The click of the handcuffs cut through the jumble of pain in Alistair's head.

"Thank you for luring him out, sir," the solider said, nodding at Alistair. "We didn't want to endanger any of the guests."

"This isn't what Gordon would've wanted," Bae pleaded as the soldier pulled him toward the truck. "He'd never want me to spend the last years of my life in prison."

"I'll have to take your word for that, uncle," Alistair replied, brushing aside the hand of the medic crouching next to him. "I only knew him for four years. But you've spent the past sixty years living with his ghost. I'm sure he'll make excellent company when they put you in solitary confinement."

As the trucks drove away, Alistair finally allowed a medic to help him to his feet. "Thank you," he said, cringing as he brushed the dust off his suit.

"Sir, we need to take you to the hospital."

"No, it's fine. I have matters to attend to here." Alistair picked his bowler hat off the ground and placed it on his head. "Family business." Trying hard to mask his limp, he walked into the hotel lobby. The next meeting of the Ekat leadership was about to start.✦

BAE OH

In 1948, Bae Oh arranged for his twin brother, Ekat leader Gordon Oh, to be killed while on a business trip in New York. Less than a week after the funeral, Bae was made head of the Ekaterina branch.

When Gordon's heartbroken wife died a few years later, Bae became the guardian of her son, Alistair. If Bae felt guilt over his actions, he didn't use his relationship with Alistair to redeem himself. Bae bullied his orphaned nephew at every opportunity, telling Alistair that he was a disappointment and a failure.

For over sixty years, Bae has led the Ekaterinas with a combination of intimidation and blackmail. When he thought that Hope Cahill and Arthur Trent were growing too powerful, he conspired with the Kabras to plot an intervention. Bae didn't worry about Hope and Arthur's two young children. He certainly didn't worry that Alistair cared deeply for Hope—that he considered her and Grace his only real family.

After returning from Ireland, Alistair Oh decided to put his uncle's reign of terror to an end. Using Madrigal contacts, he reported Bae's many illegal activities to the U.N. They sent their peacekeeping force to Cairo and arrested Bae outside the Ekat stronghold. He is currently in captivity in The Hague, awaiting trial for murder, extortion, and arms dealing. And assault and battery.

EKATERINA
TRICKS & TOOLS

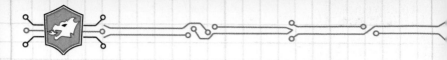

Naturally, Ekats create all the top tools and electronic tricks on the Clue hunt. They include:

MONSTER-SHAPED SUBMARINES
HALO/HAHO PARACHUTE JUMPS
SPY PENNIES
THE CLUECRAFT 3000
ROCKET SKATEBOARDS
SPY KNIVES
ALISTAIR OH'S CANE
HYPNOTISM
SECRET AGENT BOOTS

HALO /HAHO

The Tomas may have invented skydiving, but the Ekats perfected it for Clue-hunting missions. In order to break into rival strongholds, they developed the HALO (High Altitude–Low Opening) and HAHO (High Altitude–High Opening) methods. Agents brave enough to attempt a HALO jump wait until the last possible moment to open their parachutes. This dangerous move allows Ekat agents to reach such high speeds that they cannot be detected by radar. In other situations, the HAHO method is best for sneaking into enemy territory. Agents open their chutes early, which allows them to navigate through the air and land in specific locations, like the Tomas base on Alcatraz Island.

CLUECRAFT 3000

After decades of spying, the Ekats realized there was a Tomas Clue hidden somewhere in Victoria Falls—an enormous series

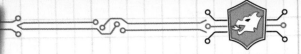

of waterfalls in southern Africa. They needed a craft that would allow them to navigate the powerful currents and explore the caves behind the wall of water. Ekat engineers used their most advanced technology to produce the Cluecraft 3000, the only boat in the world that can withstand the flow rate of the falls—over 38,000 cubic feet of water per second.

SPY PENNIES

The Ekaterinas have access to technology that the rest of the world can only imagine, such as nearly microscopic cameras and microphones that can be hidden inside a coin. Even the Kabras' surveillance bug scanner can't detect spy pennies, devices that allow the Ekats to monitor some of their most important and dangerous enemies.

LOCH NESS SUBMERSIBLE

In order to protect a Clue hidden at the bottom of Scotland's Loch Ness, the Ekats developed a submersible that looks like the legendary Loch Ness monster. It can be operated manually by an Ekat agent, or it can be programmed to patrol the water on its own, using its advanced radar and body heat sensor to detect trespassers.

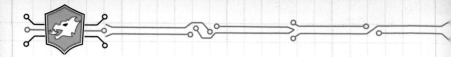

ALISTAIR OH'S CANE

More than a fashion statement, Alistair Oh's cane functions as a mobile Clue-hunting base. It contains a hidden camera, a titanium-reinforced safe for concealing stolen hints, and a black light for reading hidden messages. It's particularly useful for Alistair, as it has kept him from having to return to the Ekat stronghold on a regular basis. He preferred to avoid running into his uncle, Bae, as even the inventor of the world's most high-tech cane doesn't like to be called "useless." However, Alistair doesn't have to worry about that any longer—Bae is currently in prison facing trial for the murder of his brother, Gordon.

ROCKET SKATEBOARD

The rocket skateboard is still in its testing phase, but it promises to be one of the key Clue-hunting tools of the future, especially for young agents with good balance. It will allow agents to navigate difficult terrain and make super-speedy getaways.

SECRET AGENT BOOT

When the Tomas hid a Clue at Machu Picchu, high in the mountains of Peru, they assumed none of the other Cahills would have the bravery or stamina to find it. However, the Ekaterinas' spy boot allows them to navigate the most treacherous terrain on earth. It features a GPS navigation panel, laces that can be used as rappelling wire, and a hidden dart gun that shoots poison darts out of the toe.

EKATERINA
HOT SPOTS

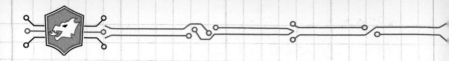

For the past 500 years, the Ekaterinas have used their advanced technology to hide Clues in some of the most secure and sneakiest locations on earth. The known Ekaterina hot spots are:

CERN	BRITISH MUSEUM, UK
SMILJAN, CROATIA	CAIRO, EGYPT
ST. PETERSBURG, RUSSIA	LUXOR, EGYPT
LOCH NESS, UK	NEW YORK CITY, USA
THE BERMUDA TRIANGLE	

ST. PETERSBURG

For centuries, the Lucians were the only Cahills in Russia. The Ekaterinas knew someone needed to balance Lucian power in the region, so they established a secret stronghold in St. Petersburg. The building is disguised as an apartment complex and is currently occupied by the Chernovs, a family of high-ranking Ekat agents. The high-security vault inside has stored a number of priceless items, including a stolen Tomas Clue—a gem cut from the same stone as the legendary Hope Diamond.

LOCH NESS

Despite their genius IQs, even the Ekats have trouble holding on to their Clues. One was almost lost during the sinking of the *Titanic*. Decades later, a plane crash landed the Clue at the bottom of Scotland's Loch Ness. Rather than risk transporting it again, the Ekats decided to leave the Clue at the bottom of the lake and came up with a unique way to protect it. They took advantage of the Loch Ness monster myth and arranged it so anyone who came too close to the Clue would be scared away by "Nessie." Little do they know that the fearsome creature is actually a monster-shaped submarine operated by a chubby Ekat agent named Charlie.

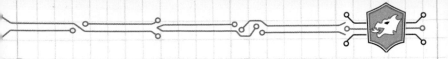

THE BERMUDA TRIANGLE

The Bermuda Triangle is one of the most mysterious spots on earth. Boats disappear without a trace. Pilots become lost and fly hundreds of miles off course. While some people point to supernatural causes, the truth is that the Ekaterinas have an ultrasecret stronghold on a small island inside the Bermuda Triangle. Their advanced security systems scramble the radar of passing boats and planes to make sure that no other Cahills ever find the island stronghold.

BRITISH MUSEUM

In the late eighteenth century, British Ekats founded a museum to house some of the treasures they discovered around the world. It was deemed the perfect place to store a new find—the Rosetta Stone, a priceless ancient Egyptian artifact that contained a crucial hint to an Ekaterina Clue. The Rosetta Stone is on public display, but the Ekats use their advanced surveillance system to keep a careful watch on all visitors. Anyone who spends a suspicious amount of time in the Egyptian gallery gets a special treat—a trip to the secret underground prison.

TOMAS

TOMAS AT A GLANCE

The Tomas are adrenaline junkies who have shaped history through their bravery and unquenchable thirst for adventure. Their enemies tend to dismiss the Tomas for being "all brawn and no brains," but that couldn't be further from the truth. The Tomas are visionaries who change the way we look at the world by discovering new lands, climbing the highest peaks, and testing the limits of human endurance. Their urge to explore new frontiers has led Tomas agents to the most extreme spots on earth and beyond—the branch has produced the world's most famous explorers, athletes, military leaders, *and* astronauts.

CREST

The Tomas symbol is the polar bear—a creature that, despite its fearsome reputation, rarely attacks unprovoked. But when it is forced to fight, the outcome is always deadly. Similarly, the Tomas prefer to use their superior strength on the playing field rather than the battlefield. But, when necessary, they turn into lethal warriors. They also appreciate the polar bear for being a stealthy hunter that often kills its prey before

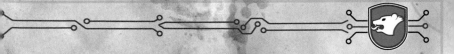

the victim ever realizes it was a target. The Tomas are still working on that part.

HISTORY

The most famous warriors in history have been Tomas, from Shaka Zulu and his fearless army to the samurai of Japan. But the Tomas don't win battles simply because they're fast and strong. They have a gift for strategy, which is why the branch boasts legendary military leaders like George Washington and the Duke of Wellington, who vanquished Napoleon.

BRANCH LEADERS

The current leader is Ivan Kleister, an extreme skier from Oslo, Norway. When he's not running meetings in Japan or South Africa, he can generally be found taking a Tomas helicopter to the top of a mountain, clipping into his skis, and jumping out.

The Tomas have a unique process for choosing their branch leaders. Anyone can nominate himself or herself for the position, but then the candidates must compete in a tournament. The first step is an iron man triathlon—a race that consists of a 2.4-mile swim, a 112-mile bike ride, and 26-mile run. The first ten to complete the event move on to the navigation/survival round. Each candidate is blindfolded and dropped, via helicopter, in a remote location such as the middle of the

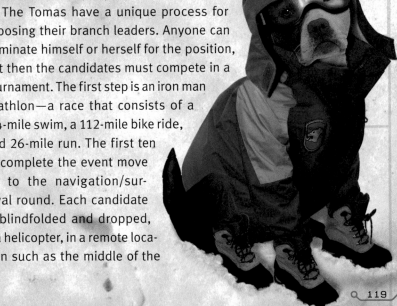

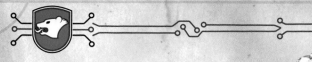

Sahara Desert or the Amazon rain forest. The first five agents to make it back to the stronghold move on to the final round—an exam on military history and strategy. In the unlikely event of a tie, the winner is determined by a chess match—played on a bed of hot coals.

STRONGHOLDS

Tomas strongholds tend to be in former military bases, such as Alcatraz Island in San Francisco Bay, or in areas that are very difficult to access, including the inside of Mount Fuji in Japan. While the Tomas use high-tech surveillance systems like the rest of the Cahills, their favorite form of security is to simply pick a spot that their rivals can't reach—like the top of treacherous mountains or in caves behind thundering waterfalls.

CHARACTERISTICS

The Tomas are the most stubborn of all the Cahill branches. As soon as you say the word "impossible," they start crafting a plan to prove you wrong. After all, it wasn't the Ekats who put the first man on the moon. The Apollo 11 mission was led by Tomas engineers and astronauts who refused to accept the impossibility of space travel.

Despite their talent for strategy, Tomas agents aren't always the sneakiest Cahills on the hunt. They believe their superior strength allows them to "break in first, ask questions later," which sometimes gets them in trouble. However, for every setback, there are countless victories—and very loud celebrations.

T O M A S
FOUNDERS

THOMAS CAHILL

Tomas founders include history's bravest explorers, most talented athletes, and boldest leaders. From George Mallory, the first person to climb Everest, to Neil Armstrong, the first man on the moon, Tomas founders have always looked for new frontiers.

SIR JOHN FRANKLIN
JEAN-BAPTISTE TAVERNIER
ANNIE OAKLEY
GERTRUDE EDERLE
BUCHANAN HOLT
GEORGE WASHINGTON
MERIWETHER LEWIS
WILLIAM CLARK
SACAGAWEA

NEIL ARMSTRONG
DAVID LIVINGSTONE
SIMÓN BOLÍVAR
ULYSSES S. GRANT
DWIGHT D. EISENHOWER
GEORGE MALLORY
MARIE MARVINGT
JESSE OWENS
KING LOUIS XIV

THOMAS CAHILL (1494–?)

As a child, Thomas Cahill, the future founder of the Tomas branch, spent countless hours with his sister Katherine, dreaming about the adventures they'd have when they grew up. Yet before they had the chance to set sail, tragedy struck. Their father, Gideon, was killed in a suspicious fire. Thomas and Katherine believed that their brother, Luke, was responsible, and that he would come after them next. When they left Ireland, Thomas and Katherine weren't in search of adventure—they were on a desperate mission to hide their Clues from Luke. They traveled to Portugal, where they'd be able to catch a ship bound for distant lands. But before they could leave, Thomas married a Portuguese woman. Angry that Thomas had chosen love over duty, Katherine fled Portugal in the middle of the night . . . taking one of Thomas's Clues with her. Thomas vowed revenge when he discovered his

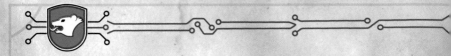

sister's treachery. He left his wife in Portugal and set off to find Katherine. Thomas's search took him to Japan, where he built the first Tomas stronghold.

ANNIE OAKLEY (1860–1926)

Annie Oakley, born Annie Mosey, grew up on a farm in Ohio when the state was part of the western frontier. Her father died when she was young, and she began hunting to help her family survive. One day, a marksman named Frank Butler came to the nearest town, offering $100 ($2,000 in today's money) to anyone who could out-shoot him. After he missed his 25th shot, Annie won. She and Frank were wed in 1882.

In 1885, Annie and Frank joined Buffalo Bill's Wild West Show and toured all over the US. Annie's talents had caught the attention of the Tomas leadership, who realized that she would excel as a Clue hunter. They arranged for the Wild West Show to tour Europe. When she wasn't performing, Annie was sent on top secret Tomas missions, such as sneaking into the Tower of London. However, Annie's fame eventually made it so her targets came to her. When she performed for the prince of Prussia, the future Kaiser Wilhelm II, she shot the butt of a cigarette hanging from his mouth. The crowd didn't know it, but the prince was a Janus and Annie was warning him off.

GEORGE WASHINGTON (1732–1799)

George Washington was the commander of the Continental army during the American Revolution and went on to become the first president of the United States. He was an

active Clue hunter in his youth but grew tired of the bloody branch rivalry. Instead, Washington used his Tomas skills in the fight for American independence. He was a brilliant general and knew how to inspire his troops, even in the worst situations. As one of the most famous Americans in history, Washington is the focus of many tall tales, such as the story about his wooden teeth. The Cahills have their own version of this mythology. Cahill children hear rumors that Washington's false teeth were actually made from different Clues like bone, tungsten, and gold. However, only part of that story is true. At one time, Washington had a set of false teeth made from hippo ivory—a material related to bone.

GEORGE MALLORY (1886–1924)

George Mallory was a British teacher and mountaineer committed to becoming the first person to reach the top of Mount Everest, the tallest mountain in the world. After two failed attempts, he and his climbing partner, Andrew Irvine, set off for a third time. Neither man returned.

Mallory was last seen just a few hundred meters from the summit. His frozen body was found on the mountain 75 years later, and experts are still debating whether he died on the way up or down. Most people believe that Mallory's obsession with climbing Everest came from his ambition and taste for adventure. However, he had an even more important reason— he was actually hiding a Clue.

Founder Archives: Annie Oakley

Annie Mosey, the future Annie Oakley, held her breath. If she made any noise, the deer would notice her and bound away through the snowy woods. Annie was small for twelve, but even her weight was enough to snap a frozen twig—and ensure that her family went hungry for another day.

She raised her rifle, resting the butt against her shoulder, just like her father had taught her. She knew that a stranger walking by would laugh at the sight of a tiny girl holding a large gun, aiming at a deer three hundred yards away. It was twilight, and her target was partially hidden by the shadows of the darkening forest. Annie smiled. She could make this shot in her sleep. She closed one eye, tensed her finger against the trigger, and then—

"Hello, there."

Startled, she raised the rifle and shot into the air. The deer streaked off. Annie whirled around and saw a tall man in an expensive-looking gray coat that seemed too tight for his muscular frame.

"Sakes alive!" she shouted, her eyes blazing with fury. "I've been tracking that deer for almost three hours. Do you know what time it is?" Without giving the intruder time to respond, she waved her rifle wildly through the air. "It's candle-lighting. Which means soon it'll be completely dark. It's too late to find any other game." She felt anger bubbling up from her empty stomach. "You owe me ten dollars, mister."

He raised his eyebrows. "Is that so?" He had traces of a foreign accent, unlike anything Annie had heard in Ohio. His clothes were even odder. She stared at the gold buttons on his coat. *Bears*, she thought.

Another man stepped out of the shadows and came to stand next to the first. He was wearing an identical coat. "This can't be the girl, Edwin," he said in an equally strange accent, a little thicker than his friend's. "She's nothing more than a child."

Edwin smiled at Annie. "Is ten dollars the price you would have received for that deer?"

"You bet your boots." She extended her arm, dirty palm face up.

Edwin chuckled. "I have a better idea. I've heard that there's quite a skilled sharpshooter in this area. Might you be the young lady?"

Annie raised her chin. "I don't set much store by gossip. But"—she smiled slightly, pleased that her reputation preceded her—"you won't find someone who can outshoot me any sooner than you can catch a weasel asleep."

The second man snickered. "Come, Edwin. We're wasting our time. This can't be the girl the leadership told us about. We must have mistranslated the code."

"Patience, Hans." He turned back to Annie. "Would you care to make a small wager?" He pointed to a tree far in the distance. "If you can hit that nest on the top bough, I'll give you your ten dollars." Annie squinted. She could barely make out the shape of the frozen mound of twigs. But she wasn't one to turn down a challenge.

In a flash, Annie hoisted her rifle onto her shoulder and took aim. There was a crack as the bullet struck the branch, and then a snap as it fell to the ground.

Both men stared at her for a moment. Edwin pulled a wad of bills from inside his coat and handed Annie ten dollars. She tucked the bills into her pocket and took a step back. "I ought to be going then."

"Hold on a moment. I'll give you a chance to double your earnings tonight." He reached back into his coat and produced a playing card. A queen of hearts. "I've been to many sharpshooting exhibitions, and I've never seen anyone put more than four bullet holes in a card." He paused. "Do you think you can do better?"

Annie took another step back. This was strange business. What kind of person spent snowy winter nights tramping through the woods, making bets? But then again, twenty dollars would be enough to feed her family for months. She took a deep breath. "I reckon I can try."

Edwin raised the card. Annie nodded to show that she was ready. He flicked it into the air and stepped back. She fired rapidly. In the corner of her eye, she could see Hans wince slightly and cover his ears. The card floated to the ground. Annie and both men stepped forward. There were six bullet holes in the card. Edwin picked it up and smiled at Hans. "I think we've found her."

He nodded. "And just in time. There's no knowing what would happen if the Ekats found out about her."

Ekats? Annie shook her head. "I don't really know what you're saying with your highfalutin accents, but I think I'd best be off." She thought about her hungry little brothers and sisters—the way the light came back into their eyes when she came home with a fresh kill or with a pocket full of coins.

"Just a moment, Annie." Edwin stepped forward.

Her head snapped up. "How do you know my name?" she asked, narrowing her eyes and raising her rifle slightly.

Edwin laughed. "It's okay. Drop your weapon."

Hans rolled his eyes. "This is why I hate recruiting agents from America. It's just a matter of time before we're shot." He paused. "Or stabbed with a pitchfork."

Edwin took another step toward Annie. "We've been looking for you for a long time, Annie. You have an incredible talent."

"A gift you're gonna see firsthand, if you don't back off," Annie warned. When he didn't move, Annie shrugged and hoisted her rifle onto her shoulder. "Fine, it's not my funeral."

"Edwin, do you need some help?" a voice called out. Six men stepped forward into the moonlit clearing. They were wearing dark gray uniforms with blue bear emblems on their jackets.

"Keep back!" Edwin ordered the newcomers. He glanced at Hans. "I *told* you we should've come alone." He turned back to Annie. "I'm sorry. This is not how I envisioned this encounter. You see, we have big plans for you, Annie. Is there somewhere we can go to talk?"

Annie had no idea who these people were or what in the blazes they wanted, but she wasn't fixing to find out.

She glanced up and scanned the trees above the uniformed men. She needed to act now, or it'd be too late. She raised her rifle and sent a series of rapid shots flying through the dark. There was a thunderous crack as a large tree bough snapped and hurtled toward the ground, bringing down smaller branches with it. There was a second of shouting followed by a chorus of groans.

Annie spun around and began sprinting toward the woods. As she ran, she could hear Edwin calling from a distance. "We'll be seeing you again, Annie. You have a great future ahead of you!"

Maybe, Annie thought as she plowed through the snow, panting as she made her way up a snowy hill. *But it ain't gonna be with no bear-obsessed foreigners.* At the top, she paused and looked behind her. Hers were the only footprints she could see. She took a deep breath and slipped her hand into the pocket. The bills were still there. Her family would have enough to eat until spring. She exhaled and then set her lips together firmly. And she'd sleep with one eye open, in case those bear men were foolish enough to come calling. ❖

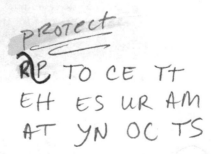

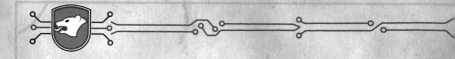

SHAKA ZULU (c. 1787–c. 1828)

Shaka was a Zulu warrior famous for his strategy. Instead of throwing spears from a distance like other Zulu fighters, Shaka used short spears that caused deadlier wounds. Shaka also came up with the famous buffalo horn attack. He divided his troops up into three groups, the first charging their enemies head-on. While Shaka's foes were fighting off these attackers, the other two groups sneaked around to strike at both flanks. Few could withstand a tangle with Shaka's buffalo horns.

Shaka's leadership talents allowed him to create the first Zulu nation. Yet he had even bigger ambitions. When an Englishman named Henry Francis Fynn arrived in the Zulu kingdom, Shaka saw the opportunity to increase his power. Fynn was a Tomas who had traveled to Africa looking for a plant needed for the Tomas serum. In return for helping to find the plant, Fynn promised to bring Shaka into the Tomas branch and share a tiny sip of the last remaining vial of Tomas serum.

Shaka became a Tomas agent and the guardian of the Aloe Clue. He gave orders for the Clue to be buried with him so that he could continue to protect it from the grave. Tomas warriors don't let a little thing like death stand in the way of duty.

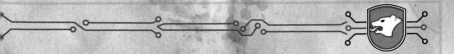

TOYOTOMI HIDEYOSHI (1536–1598)

Historians are puzzled by Japanese warrior Toyotomi Hideyoshi. Very little is known about his early life. It almost seems as if he appeared by magic. However, Tomas agents know the truth: Hideyoshi was the son of Thomas Cahill.

Thomas Cahill arrived in Japan around 1514. After he learned of the death of his first wife, Thomas married a Japanese woman named Keiko, with whom he had four more children. Thomas knew this family would never be safe from his brother, Luke. The only way to protect his children was to train them to be warriors.

His son, Hideyoshi, grew up to be a powerful warlord and ruled Japan as the imperial regent. However, he knew it was only a matter of time before his Cahill cousins made it to Japan to hunt for Thomas's Clues. Hideyoshi adopted a strict policy about outsiders and even ordered the execution of western missionaries, in case they were secretly Cahills.

As further protection, Hideyoshi forbade peasants from owning swords, and he confiscated weapons from around the country. Most people believe that the swords were melted down to create a statue of Buddha, but top Tomas agents know that Hideyoshi actually sent the swords to a secret cave in Korea along with an even more precious item— a Tomas Clue.

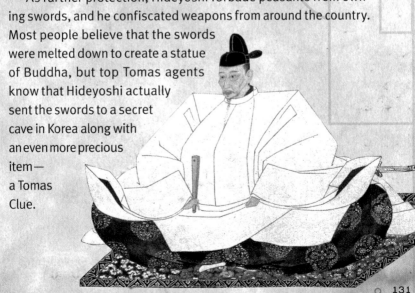

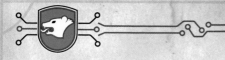

BUCHANAN HOLT
(1931–1982)

As a young man, Buchanan Holt was the golden boy of the Tomas branch. He was an All-American football player and won a gold medal in the 1948 Olympics for rowing. He was also a top agent. In 1952, he qualified for the Olympics in speed-skating. However, Buchanan never got to make history by medalling in both Summer and Winter Games.

BUCHANAN HOLT
1931 – 1982
CHAMPION ATHLETE, TRAITOR

That year, the Tomas leadership accused Buchanan of leaking crucial branch secrets to the Ekats. Buchanan had been chosen to transport a highly sensitive file from the Mount Fuji stronghold to South Africa—something too important to send in the mail. A few days later, the same document appeared in the Ekat stronghold in Cairo.

Buchanan denied the charges, but the proof was hard to ignore. If the Ekats had stolen the document themselves, they would have bragged about it. But they were as confused as the Tomas. No one ever suspected that there was an outside group devoted to causing discord within the Cahill family—a group that had been shadowing the branches for centuries.

Buchanan was barred from the hunt. By the time his son, Eisenhower, was born, the Holt name was associated with treachery. Desperate to protect his son from a similar fate, Buchanan became obsessed with turning Eisenhower into a top agent and Clue hunter, just as he had been. However, after Buchanan's wife died, he found it increasingly difficult to communicate with his young son. Their relationship was strained until the end of Buchanan's life.

T O M A S
AGENTS

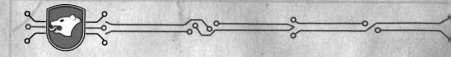

Some Tomas agents apply their superior athletic skills to the Clue hunt. Others use their talents to achieve superstardom in soccer matches or at lumberjack competitions. But whether they're kicking a ball, felling a tree, or breaking into an enemy stronghold, one thing remains the same: The Tomas are always the fastest, strongest, and loudest ones around.

GEORGE MCCLAIN
PAUL ADDISON
HEINRICH HEINRICHSON
HAMILTON HOLT
REAGAN HOLT
MADISON HOLT

EISENHOWER HOLT
MARY-TODD HOLT
IVAN KLEISTER
HERBERT MALUSI
ANDREW BHEKISISA
MALEIA KALANI

EISENHOWER HOLT

Almost everything about Eisenhower Holt is supersized. His feet. His biceps. His temper. And his intense desire to prove himself to the Tomas branch. As a child, Eisenhower dreamed about becoming a top Clue hunter. He covered his wall with a map and marked all the known Clue locations, as well as those he suspected. He was right about the Lucian Clue in Area 51. His theory about the Janus Clue in the paint section of a Milwaukee Home Depot? Not so much.

However, Eisenhower's opportunities were limited. His father, Buchanan, had been accused of leaking top secret information to the Ekaterinas. After that, no one would trust Buchanan or his family. Eisenhower believed his father had been framed and grew up committed to redeeming the Holt name. Yet he encountered more bad luck at West Point. When Buchanan came to visit, Eisenhower was so excited to show off his rifle that he forgot about the rule forbidding cadets from taking their weapons off

campus. Eisenhower's roommate, Arthur Trent, reported him to the Superintendent, and Eisenhower was expelled.

After years of disappointments, Eisenhower saw the Clue hunt as his last chance to make a name for himself. He was willing to do whatever necessary to crush the competition. However, when his son, Hamilton, emerged from the Madrigal stronghold, Eisenhower didn't care that he had given up their Clues. He realized the respect of your branch is nothing compared to the love of your son.

IVAN KLEISTER

Ivan Kleister is a champion hockey player. He's a legendary boxer. And he's one of the best extreme skiers on the planet. However, his leadership skills aren't quite as powerful as his terrifying right hook. Although he has no trouble making a split-second decision on the ice or in the air, he's not as confident when it comes to Clue-hunting strategy. Rather than make the *wrong* decision, sometimes Ivan prefers to make none at all. He's committed to the Tomas cause and is desperate for them to find the Clues, but he's more comfortable arranging a volleyball tournament than he is a worldwide treasure hunt. Yet the classic Tomas in him refuses to admit defeat. Whenever something goes wrong, he looks for someone else to blame.

PAUL ADDISON

Paul Addison lives in Drumnadrochit, Scotland, near the famous Loch

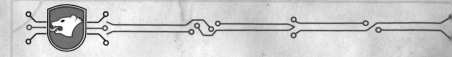

Ness. He used to spend his summers hiding from the tourists who flocked to the town hoping for a "Nessie" sighting. He hated their huge cameras. He despised the monster-shaped water bottles they bought at the souvenir stand. And he couldn't bear Charlie Wallace, the man who ran the "Nessie Shack" and gave tours of the loch. There was something a little off—as if the chubby, cheery guide were hiding more than a beer gut. Paul decided to investigate, and soon things began to get ugly. But despite the Ekat leadership's best efforts, this young Tomas was responsible for exposing one of the biggest conspiracies in Cahill history—the fact that "Nessie" was actually an Ekat submarine protecting a Clue.

MALEIA KALANI

Growing up in Hawaii, Maleia had limited opportunities to go on Clue-hunting missions. However, whenever she wasn't surfing, Maleia devoted herself to researching potential Clue locations around the world. She was one of the only agents from any branch to suspect Cahill activity on Easter Island. After winning a number of surfing competitions in Hawaii and California, Maleia qualified for a tournament in Tahiti. She convinced her sponsor to let her fly through Easter Island on her return trip and became the first Cahill to get within 2,000 miles of the Madrigal stronghold. She couldn't find the moai that conceals the hidden entrance, which is probably for the best. There's no knowing what the Madrigals would have been forced to do if a Tomas had discovered their secret.

THE HOLT KIDS

AGES: 11–15
BRANCH: TOMAS
HOMETOWN:
MILWAUKEE, USA

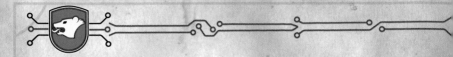

THE HOLT KIDS

In their Milwaukee suburb, the Holt kids are public enemies one, two, and three. (The order switches depending on the season and which Holt kid is currently playing a sport that involves large wooden sticks.) Yet while they have the reputation for being bullies, the truth is that they simply never learned how to interact with other kids. A six-year-old who can tackle members of the high school football team is always going to have trouble on the playground.

Their father didn't make things any easier for them. Eisenhower was obsessed with turning his children into champions—a family of top athletes and star Clue hunters that would change the way the Tomas branch thought of the Holts. As soon as they could walk, the Holt kids began an intense training regimen that included 4 a.m. runs, 6 a.m. weight lifting sessions, and weekends spent hiking, mountain climbing, or competing in lumberjack tournaments.

However, things have changed since the Holts returned from the Clue hunt. The kids are no longer terrified of their father. Hamilton felt comfortable joining the computer club and, after the first few weeks, the other members stopped hiding when he came into the room. Reagan confessed that she'd been taking ballet class. With the secret out, Reagan could invite her family to her performance of *Swan Lake*. The Holts enjoyed watching Reagan out-leap and out-twirl every girl in the class. Madison is finally starting to learn that you can't trash-talk the other dancers . . . though they're still trying to teach Arnold the dog the difference between real swans and girls in tutus.

Agent Update: Hamilton Holt

"Madison, stop smiling," Eisenhower Holt ordered as they stopped for a Powerbar break. Hamilton looked over and saw his sister grinning from under the hood of her purple parka as she posed for their mother's camera.

After more than four hours of hiking, the Holts were nearing the top of Mount Fuji. The Japanese countryside had disappeared and all they could see around them was blue sky and fluffy white clouds.

"You need to work on your game face," Eisenhower shouted as a gust of wind swept over them. "We have to enter the stronghold like champions." A determined look crossed his face, an expression Hamilton recognized from when Eisenhower tried to program the DVR.

Hamilton felt a twinge of now-familiar anxiety. Ever since William McIntyre had asked the Holts to convince some Tomas to join the Madrigal cause, he'd felt like a weight had been placed on his chest. And as they climbed up Mount Fuji, it only grew heavier. For the past 500 years, no Tomas agent had ever pulled out of a basketball game, let alone the Clue hunt. And now the Holts—the branch outcasts—were supposed to show up and convince them to switch sides?

"How much farther is it, sugar maple?" Mary-Todd asked.

Eisenhower looked up. "Well, the stronghold is 1700 meters above the Fujinomiya station." He turned to scan their surroundings. "And the sun sets in the west." He scratched his head as he looked up at the sky. "But we're in the eastern hemisphere, so that means, erm, you have to divide everything by two—"

"Hey!" Madison shouted. "Look at this!" She pointed to an abstract image carved into the rock. It looked vaguely like a four-legged animal. "I didn't know they had moose in Japan." She

leaned closer. "Mom, take my picture!" She smiled widely.

"Madison! *No* smiling."

Hamilton took a step forward and squinted. "I don't think that's a moose."

But Madison was busy arguing with Eisenhower. "Dad, get out of the way. I want a picture with the moose!"

"*Fine.* But put on your game face!"

"But moose make me happy! Remember that time we were camping and I saw that baby moose and I was like 'hi, baby moose' and then the mama moose came over—"

"Hold on," Hamilton shouted. "It's. Not. A—"

"And then we had to bribe the park ranger to let us—"

"It's a BEAR!" Hamilton yelled. He took a deep breath, realizing that once he spoke, there would be no going back. "We found the entrance."

The tunnel was lined with portraits of famous Tomas agents. George Washington. Annie Oakley. LeBron James. They reached the end and, one at a time, pressed their hands against the fingerprint scanner next to the door. It slid open and they walked in.

Hamilton gasped. They were standing on a balcony, looking over the largest indoor space he'd ever seen—at least ten times larger than a football stadium. Below them were soccer fields, basketball courts, and gymnastic rooms. Beyond that were running tracks, boxing rings, and what looked like a go-kart course. He felt his stomach tighten as he surveyed the intense concentration on the agents' faces. They weren't the type to be sympathetic to a fifteen-year-old kid who had made the impromptu decision to share the branch's Clues.

"*Look!*" Madison shouted. Hamilton turned and saw the entire side of the stronghold was made up of a giant indoor ski slope, complete with snow machines and a chair lift. Skiers and snowboarders were zooming down the different runs or catching air in the giant half pipe.

One of the skiers was even faster than the rest, streaking down the nearly vertical slope in a straight line. He flew over the lip of a jump and caught so much air that he actually flew out of the ski area. Hamilton watched as he hurled through the air toward them, landing with a heavy thump on the balcony.

He was a tall blond man with deeply tanned skin and icy blue eyes. Although he was strapped into a pair of high performance skis, his stance was relaxed and confident. "Welcome, Holt family," he said in a slight Norwegian accent.

Eisenhower threw back his shoulders. "Hello, Ivan."

The noise level in the stronghold had decreased dramatically. Hamilton noticed that the people on the fields below had stopped their games and were staring up at them.

"You have perfect timing. I just got back from the South African stronghold. I had to oversee some personnel changes."

Hamilton saw a flash of concern on Eisenhower's face. "Malusi's not in charge there anymore?"

"No." Ivan shook his head. "Unfortunately, Mr. Malusi's current condition prevents him from performing those duties."

"What happened?" Mary-Todd asked.

Ivan smiled, revealing dazzling white teeth.

"He allowed the Cahill children to steal a Clue. We can't let that kind of negligence go unpunished."

Hamilton cleared his throat and stepped forward. He had to be the one to break the news. "Umm, excuse me, Ivan?" he began. "I was wondering if I could, um, speak to everyone here."

Ivan cast his icy gaze on Hamilton. "And this must be the young man who *gave* Amy and Dan his Clues. Of course you can address the stronghold," he said with mock enthusiasm. "Will you be giving an inspiring lecture about how to give up?" He

sneered. "After all, you're the only Tomas with any first hand experience of being a pathetic quitter."

"How *dare* you?" Eisenhower's face was turning purple. He took a step toward Ivan, but Mary-Todd pulled him back.

"Not now, melon ball," she said, digging her heels into the floor.

All other activity in the stronghold had ceased. A crowd had formed below the balcony. Even the skiers had stopped to watch and were trying to keep themselves from slipping down the slope.

"If you'd just give me a chance to explain," Hamilton started.

"*Explain?*" Ivan spat, taking a step forward. "You have an *explanation* for why you gave up our Clues? Why you became the worst traitor in Tomas history since your grandfather?" Hamilton heard his father gasp.

"Hey! Guy with the scary eyes?" Madison called out. "You know what a moose does when someone insults her family?"

Ivan raised his eyebrows.

"She does this." Madison crouched down and charged Ivan. Her head hit him in the stomach. Teetering in his skis, he flailed his arms in an attempt to catch his balance, but it was too late. With a yelp, he staggered backward over the balcony rail. Hamilton rushed over and saw Ivan fall through the air, landing with a heavy thud on a stack of gymnastic mats.

Gasps and murmurs echoed through the stronghold. Hamilton started edging toward the door. Would the agents try to grab them? Suddenly, a voice called down from below. "*We* want to hear what happened." He took a step forward and peeked over the balcony. The crowd was looking up at him with a mix of expressions on their faces. Confusion. Anger. Curiosity. Excitement. But none of them were poised to charge him with a baseball bat. Hamilton took a deep breath. It was game time. ❧

TOMAS
TRICKS & TOOLS

It's easy to see how Tomas talents translate into Clue-hunting skills. Their athleticism and bravery allow them to hide Clues in treacherous locations. And their strength enables them to fight off even their sneakiest enemies. However, the Tomas have lesser-known talents that also factor into their success. Their tolerance for pain allows agents to cover their bodies with tattoos—an ideal place for hiding important hints! The Tomas are also great with animals, which makes them excellent cowboys . . . or spy sea lion trainers. Tomas tricks and tools include:

TATTOO CODES	MARTIAL ARTS
PARKOUR	SPY SEA LIONS
SHURIKEN CODES	MOUNTAINEERING
URBAN CLIMBING	EXPLORATION
SCOREBOARD CODES	SAMURAI SKILLS
NAVIGATION SKILLS	HORSEBACK RIDING

URBAN CLIMBING/PARKOUR

When the Tomas want to break into another branch's stronghold, they don't waste time studying heating system blueprints or arranging elaborate disguises. They simply use their urban climbing skills to scale the building. Tomas can climb anything: monuments, statues, bridges—even skyscrapers! Recently, the branch leadership sent agents to climb the Eiffel Tower to find a Lucian Clue. They made it to the top easily but, unfortunately, the Clue had been temporarily moved to the Statue of Liberty.

Of course, not every mission goes quite so smoothly. When

the Tomas have to make a quick getaway, they use parkour—a series of leaps, jumps, and other acrobatic moves that allows agents to race through urban environments. Parkour experts can even jump over cars, over walls, and across roofs, although special training is required for these highly dangerous stunts.

EXPLORATION

Like their founder, Thomas Cahill, members of the Tomas branch are famous for their wanderlust. They crave adventure and get a thrill from exploring distant shores. Their passion for discovering new lands has shaped history, as Tomas explorers have been the first to reach the North Pole, the South Pole, the top of Mount Everest, and the surface of the moon. The Tomas's adventurous spirit also gives them an edge over their competition. Their Clues are often the best protected, as they hide them in places no one could possibly access—like the ocean's deepest trench.

HORSEBACK RIDING

The Tomas's talent for horseback riding has been a crucial part of their Clue-hunting successes. For centuries, the best warriors were also the boldest riders, as they were the most effective on the battlefield. In the 19th century, Tomas horsemanship allowed them to dominate the American West. The Tomas bandits could outride and outshoot anyone, including law enforcement, which made

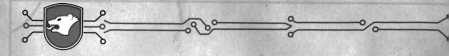

them the most powerful branch west of the Mississippi. However, law-abiding agents were also important. Most Pony Express riders were Tomas, which gave them access to all the messages sent throughout the West—even the coded ones.

SPY SEA LIONS

Although the Tomas are amazing athletes, they know that their skills have limits. The most experienced scuba diver is no match for a pair of built-in flippers, supercharged senses, and ridiculously cute whiskers. Tomas in the military use sea lions to detect bombs, deliver equipment, and watch for enemy divers. The US Navy has even trained the animals to attach leg cuffs to intruders and pull them back to their handlers for questioning.

The Tomas also use spy sea lions for their Clue-hunting operations. Special sea lion agents patrol the waters around important Tomas locations—like the area above the Mariana Trench—making it difficult for rival Cahills to sneak in undetected. They can also be used to spy on the other branches. The Tomas attach underwater cameras to the sea lions' harnesses and then send them to take photos of enemy territories.

TOMAS
HOT SPOTS

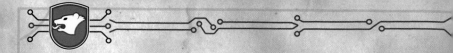

Tomas hot spots tend to fall into two categories: They're remote spots perfect for hiding Clues, like the Canadian Arctic. Or they're home to extreme sporting events, like Teahupo'o, where the world's most famous surfing competitions are held. Tomas hot spots include:

MONUMENT VALLEY, USA
ALCATRAZ ISLAND, USA
SOUTH KOREA
MACHU PICCHU, PERU
MARIANA TRENCH
WEST POINT, USA
NORTH POLE/CANADIAN ARCTIC
NATIONAL PALACE, MEXICO

WAIMEA BAY, USA
IDITAROD ROUTE, USA
TEAHUPO'O, TAHITI
OLYMPIC SITES
MOUNT FUJI, JAPAN
SOUTH AFRICA
VICTORIA FALLS, AFRICA
TOKYO, JAPAN

OLYMPIC SITES

It takes years for the International Olympic Committee (IOC) to choose a city to host the Olympic Games. The voting is done in secret and it's difficult to determine why IOC members make the decisions they do. Only Cahill insiders know the truth: The Olympics are run by the Tomas, and the IOC chooses locations based on their Clue-hunting strategy. The 2000 Games were held in Sydney so Tomas agents could search for Amelia Earhart's lost Clue. During the 2008 Olympics in Beijing, the Tomas were on the lookout for Janus Emperor Puyi's Clue. Now that the hunt is over, the cities that have been snubbed for decades will have their chance. Get excited, Cleveland.

MOUNT FUJI

The Ekats like to pretend that the Tomas aren't as technologically

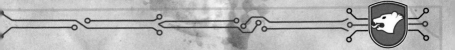

advanced as the rest of the Cahills. Bae Oh once spread a rumor that Ivan Kleister has to keep a Post-it note attached to his TV remote to remind him what the different buttons do. However, the Tomas's stronghold in Japan's Mount Fuji suggests otherwise. It takes a lot of smarts to build a secret base inside a mountain, especially one with an indoor ski slope. The Tomas are also great at mixing business with pleasure. After intense branch meetings in the Mount Fuji stronghold, Tomas agents wind down with a relaxing ultimate fighting tournament or a soothing rugby match. Of course, it's not all fun and games. The surveillance center inside the stronghold operates 24 hours a day, monitoring Cahill hot spots all over the world.

ALCATRAZ ISLAND

In the 19th century, power in the American West was determined by who could ride the fastest, shoot the straightest, and look the meanest. Naturally, the Tomas ran the show. Their main base of operations in the Wild West was Alcatraz Island, in San

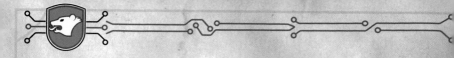

Francisco Bay. Originally a military fort and then a federal prison, Alcatraz has always been Tomas owned and operated. The remote island surrounded by chilly, shark-infested waters was also the perfect place to hide a Clue. Before the island's prison was shut down, the Tomas loved to imprison their rivals in "the Rock." The inmates often went mad knowing how frustratingly close they were to a Tomas Clue.

WEST POINT

The United States Military Academy at West Point has been dominated by the Tomas since it was founded in 1802. The academy has produced two Tomas presidents: the Civil War hero Ulysses S. Grant and Dwight D. Eisenhower, who led the Allied forces to victory in World War II. Admission is so difficult that even Tomas sometimes have trouble getting in. Cadets need to be nominated by their congressman, which is hard for Tomas who live in districts controlled by Lucians. In addition to providing an awesome military education, West Point is also ideal for anyone who wants to spy on the Tomas . . . like the group that sent Arthur Trent as a cadet in the 1980s.

TEAHUPO'O

Teahupo'o is a legendary surf spot off the coast of Tahiti, an island in French Polynesia. The enormous waves attract surfers from around the world, which makes Teahupo'o a hotbed of Tomas activity. It's where the Tomas perfected "tow-in surfing," a technique that allows surfers to catch waves that are too big and fast to paddle out to. In the tow-in method, surfers are towed to a wave by a jet ski or helicopter. Cahills from other branches like to watch from the beach, hoping for a massive Tomas wipeout. However, more often than not, these visitors leave feeling pretty

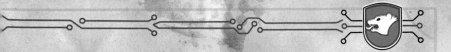

worried about the Clue hunt. After watching Tomas agents surf at Teahupo'o, it's clear that the branch is totally fearless.

VICTORIA FALLS

In 1866, the Scottish missionary and explorer David Livingstone set out to find the source of the Nile River. At least, that's what most of the world believed. Cahills suspected that he was actually looking for a new hiding place for a Tomas Clue—somewhere deep in the African jungle. Livingstone lost contact with the outside world for several years.

Eager to discover Livingstone's secret, the Janus sent reporter Henry Morton Stanley to Africa to follow him. Stanley eventually found Livingstone, but the Clue was already safely hidden in a cave behind Victoria Falls—a series of enormous waterfalls on the border of Zambia and Zimbabwe. For years, the other branches have tried to figure out a way to retrieve the Clue. The Ekats even designed a special boat to navigate the roiling waters beneath the falls, though they're having trouble finding volunteers to pilot it.

JANUS

A JONAH WIZARD PRODUCTION KNOWS DIRECTOR LESLIE D. MILL WHERE EXECUTIVE PRODUCER BRODERICK WIZARD IT PRODUCER IS AMLA COHN-ORBACH

JANUS AT A GLANCE

For the past 500 years, the world's most accomplished and creative artists have been members of the Janus branch. They include innovative painters like Vincent van Gogh, acclaimed writers like Jane Austen, visionary musicians like Wolfgang Amadeus Mozart, celebrated actors like Daniel Radcliffe, and many more.

Yet Janus talents extend beyond painting and music. Their creativity allows agents to excel at more competitive activities, like martial arts and stunt flying. Their imagination also gives them an edge over their Clue-hunting rivals. The flying ace Raoul Gervais Lufbery was a Janus agent who used his ingenuity to fly circles around enemy pilots during the First World War.

STRATEGY

The Janus are just as passionate about art as they are about finding the 39 Clues. They believe it makes the world a better place, and that the power of the Clues will allow them to make art the focus of every society on earth.

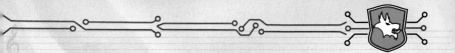

Some of the most famous works of art in the world were actually created as part of the hunt for the 39 Clues. The inspiration for Mary Shelley's book *Frankenstein* came during a meeting of top Janus agents in Switzerland at the beginning of the 19th century, and Shelley even hid a Clue in the text of the novel.

While the Janus have the reputation for being peaceful dreamers, they can be just as dangerous as the other branches of the Cahill family. Janus leaders throughout history have placed artistic creation above the needs of their people, letting their subjects starve while building lavish palaces and ornate monuments. The Janus are also willing to use the same brutal Clue-hunting methods as their peers—Janus agents use swords as skillfully as they used quill pens.

BRANCH LEADERS

Until the 19th century, the branch was run by one elected leader. This system wasn't ideal for the creative and often impulsive Janus. Sometimes, the branch head would have a "flash of inspiration" and would disappear for days as he or she worked on a painting or composed a sonata. The Janus realized that it would be better to have three leaders at a time, to share responsibility and balance out any eccentric personalities.

The current leaders had been Cora Wizard, Halima Amad, and Spencer Langodeon. However, Cora found the "trifecta" system inefficient. She believed that in order for the Janus to beat the other branches, they needed one strong leader to make decisions.

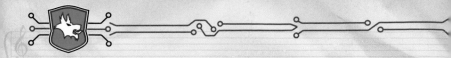

Shortly after she was elected, Cora found a way to gain the power she craved. She bribed Halima to quit and, when Spencer resisted, Cora leaked fake documents that made it look like Spencer had plagiarized his award-winning book of poetry. He resigned in disgrace.

BRANCH CREST

It is fitting that the symbol of the Janus branch is the wolf—an animal that embodies elegance and wisdom. However, while peaceful wolves are beautiful creatures, they can be vicious killers when necessary.

STRONGHOLDS

The main Janus stronghold is in Los Angeles, hidden under the famed Hollywood sign. There is another important stronghold in Venice, Italy, where the Janus store priceless works of art and crucial Clue-related evidence. Janus influence around the world can also be seen in the countless buildings and monuments designed by Janus architects, from Spain's La Sagrada Familia to the Hagia Sophia in Istanbul.

Choice 3

JANUS
FOUNDERS

Jane Cahill

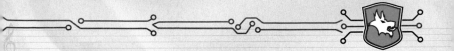

The Janus are champion multitaskers. Who says you can't write operas *and* search for Clues? And just because someone is a world-famous actress, it doesn't mean she can't also be a secret agent. Throughout history, Janus agents have balanced brilliant careers with sneaky Clue-hunting activities. They include:

THOMAS JEFFERSON   EMPEROR MAXIMILIAN OF MEXICO
JANE CAHILL   LUDWIG II OF BAVARIA
ALESSANDRO CAGLIOSTRO   AMBROSE BIERCE
HARRY HOUDINI   SIR WALTER RALEIGH
GERVAIS RAOUL LUFBERY   JOSEPHINE BAKER
HENRY MORTON STANLEY   CHARLIE CHAPLIN
GEORGE, LORD BYRON   HEDY LAMARR
JOHN KEATS   JAMES DEAN
MARY SHELLEY   MARK TWAIN
PERCY BYSSHE SHELLEY   NANNERL MOZART
JANE AUSTEN   EMPEROR PUYI OF CHINA
VINCENT VAN GOGH   WOLFGANG AMADEUS MOZART

JANE CAHILL (1497–?)

Ten-year-old Jane Cahill—the future founder of the Janus branch—was devastated when her older brother Luke fled Ireland. Despite the evidence, she couldn't believe that her favorite brother could have started the fire that killed their father. When she realized that Luke was missing, Jane sprinted to the dock to catch him, but it was too late. Her favorite brother had abandoned her. Jane knew she could never return home. Although she felt guilty about leaving her mother, she was suffocating on their small island. She wanted to explore her talents in an inspiring environment. However, Jane soon realized that it was just as difficult for a girl to make it as

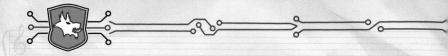

an artist in London as it was on an island in the Irish Sea. Women weren't taken seriously as writers and musicians, let alone young girls from Ireland. Unable to find anyone to publish her poetry or let her perform with her harp, Jane began posing as a boy. Without the distraction of her gender, her talent could speak for itself. Within a few years, Jane—or John—was one of London's biggest stars.

SIR WALTER RALEIGH (1552–1618)

Poets were the rock stars of the 17th century, and Walter Raleigh was the most rebellious of them all. An explorer and a known pirate, Raleigh was also a devoted Clue hunter and became the first Janus to successfully steal a Lucian Clue. He knew it would never be safe in England, so he spirited it away to the New World. Raleigh arranged for a group of colonists to settle on Roanoke Island (in present-day Virginia) thousands of miles away from the nearest Lucian stronghold. A few years later, a ship sailed from England to find that the entire colony had disappeared—setting the stage for one of the greatest unsolved mysteries in history. But Cahill insiders know the truth: The Lucians tracked their stolen Clue across the ocean and destroyed the colony. Then they conspired to have Raleigh imprisoned in the Tower of London. He was executed in 1618.

JOSEPHINE BAKER (1906–1975)

As Jonah Wizard knows, sometimes celebrities make the best spies. Josephine Baker was an American-born singer, dancer, and actress who moved to France and became one of the most popular entertainers in history. When World War II broke out, Baker joined the French Resistance, smuggling crucial information out of France in her sheet music. In addition to supporting

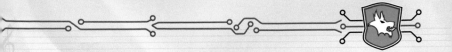

the Resistance, Baker used her spy skills to help the Janus. When the Lucians decided it would be safer to move one of their Clues out of war-torn Europe, Baker was sent to intercept it. The Lucian agent transporting the Clue was so flustered by the sight of his favorite singer that Baker was able to steal the treasure right out from under his nose.

LUDWIG II OF BAVARIA (1845–1886)

Mad King Ludwig of Bavaria loved music and was passionate about the work of composer Richard Wagner. He even decorated one of his lavish palaces, Neuschwanstein Castle, with scenes from Wagner's operas. Ludwig became famous for his castle-designing frenzy—he nearly bankrupted his country by building fantasy palaces throughout his kingdom. Linderhof Palace featured an indoor lake where the king could be rowed around in a shell-shaped boat.

Ludwig's enemies tried to make the king look insane, but he had a good reason for building his palaces. Ludwig was in charge of protecting a Janus Clue, and he knew the extra buildings would serve as red herrings. Ludwig was wise to take these precautions. In 1886, he died under mysterious circumstances—his body was found on the shores of a lake.

Founder Archives: Raoul Lufbery

Gervais Raoul Lufbery opened the flap to his tent and rolled his eyes. You could say a lot about lions, but they certainly weren't early risers. Whiskey was still fast asleep in bed.

"Whiskey. Wake up," he said softly. The cub didn't stir. "Whiskey. *Réveille-toi*," he said slightly louder. Whiskey responded by opening one eye, blinking lazily a few times, and then closing it again.

It was nearly noon, and the tent's canvas walls did little to block the noise from outside: the rhythmic thud of boots, the rumble of ambulances bringing the wounded back from the trenches, and in the distance, the patter of gunfire. Yet Whiskey was stretched out on the bed like a guest in a four-star hotel.

"Fine," Raoul said, stuffing his arms into his bomber jacket. "I guess I'll go on this mission by myself."

Whiskey's ears pricked up. He raised his head and tilted it to the side.

"That's right," Raoul said, walking over to scratch the lion's fuzzy head. Whiskey closed his eyes and flattened his ears so Raoul could reach his itchy spots. "We've got a job to do. *Allons-y.*" Whiskey sat up and yawned. He raised his enormous paw, gave it a few licks, and then swiped it across his face. He looked at Raoul expectantly.

"Very handsome," he said, nodding his approval. He grabbed a pair of aviator goggles from his trunk, walked over to the bed, and fitted them on Whiskey's head. "Let's go."

Whiskey jumped down and followed Raoul out of the tent. A passing soldier gave a yelp as he saw Whiskey and leaped to the side. "I'm not sure I'm ever going to get used to him, Lufbery," he said, shaking his head. "Why can't you just get a dog?"

Raoul smiled. "Because wrestling a lion for blankets makes fighting Germans seem like a treat."

Raoul walked briskly through the maze of canvas tents with Whiskey trotting at his heels. The camp was a flurry of activity. Smoke rose from makeshift kitchens, officers were shouting orders, and soldiers ran in all directions.

"*Salut*, Whiskey!" a lieutenant called out. "*Ça va bien?*"

"Hiya, Whiskey," an American pilot said as he jogged past. "Hope you like kaiser meat, 'cause I'm gonna bring you some real soon."

"*Mais oui*, Pete," Raoul said. "As soon as you learn to tell the front of the plane from the back." He grinned. "Let me know if you need any help."

As he and Whiskey approached the hospital tent, his smile faded. Stretchers were lined up along the road. Some of the soldiers were awake, trying to keep their spirits up by joking with their neighbors. Others were in much more serious condition. Raoul averted his eyes as he passed a man groaning. Blood was seeping through the dressings on his thigh—a bandage that stopped ominously above the knee. The next few soldiers had gauze wrapped around their eyes. *Mustard gas*, Raoul thought to himself. The man on the last stretcher had no visible injuries, but his face was white and he lay perfectly still. A passing orderly reached down to feel the man's pulse. He shook his head and then pulled a blanket over the body.

Raoul felt his stomach tighten. He had thought going to war would be the ultimate adventure and the best way to look for Clues. He had been right about the second part. But the war was no adventure. Just an endless stream of suffering and a tragic waste of young lives.

That's why we have to find the Clues first. There wouldn't be any wars in a world under Janus control. People would be united by their love of art, whether in the form of painting, music, books, or the beauty of a perfectly executed airplane stunt.

Raoul walked onto the field where his unit kept their planes.

Georges, one of the mechanics, was inspecting a propeller on Raoul's plane. "*Bonjour*, Raoul. *Bonjour*, Whiskey," Georges said as they approached. "I thought you had the day off."

"Just going to practice a few moves," he answered casually. "Don't worry. I'll bring her back in one piece."

"You always do." Georges smiled.

Raoul climbed into the cockpit and started the engine. As the propellers began to spin, he whistled loudly, and Whiskey sprang into the seat behind them. A few minutes later, man and lion were airborne.

Soon they were flying over smooth green fields unmarked by the trenches that scarred most of the western front. He glanced down at the dashboard and then back up at the horizon. For a moment, Raoul felt an unfamiliar twinge of nervousness. It was one thing to fly circles around a few Germans. It was quite another to fly into the center of Paris. Even if no one tried to shoot him down, it would be difficult to keep this mission secret. No one would believe that France's most celebrated pilot had gotten that lost.

"You ready, Whiskey?" he shouted, glancing over his shoulder. The cub's eyes were closed and the wind was streaming over his face, pushing back his fur and lifting his jowls to reveal black lips.

The houses below them were growing more numerous and, in the distance, the Parisian skyline came into focus. Raoul could make out the top of Notre Dame, the Arc de Triomphe, and there, dominating the cityscape, the spire of the Eiffel Tower.

The Janus had always suspected Gustave Eiffel's real reason for designing the structure. The leadership believed there was a Clue hidden at the top, and it was Raoul's job to find it.

He began to descend, dropping altitude until he could make out the shapes of the carriages and the color of the shop awnings. He turned and began circling the tower, aware that the people in the park below were beginning to point.

He spiraled in, bringing his circle even closer to the tower. As he approached the top of the spire, Raoul banked so the plane was almost perpendicular to the ground. "Go!" he shouted. Whiskey rose from the seat, placed his paws on the edge of the plane, and leaped, landing on one of the tower's support beams.

Over the roar of the engine and the rush of the wind, Raoul could hear faint screams from the people on the observation deck. He circled around again. By the time he returned, Whiskey was perched on a beam, holding something in his mouth. As Raoul flew by, Whiskey jumped into the plane and they took off, zooming away from the city as quickly as they had come.

"Good boy, Whiskey!" Raoul shouted. Once they were a safe distance away, he reached behind and pulled the item from Whiskey's mouth. His heart fell. It was just a piece of paper, damp with lion spit. He glanced down and saw a series of letters written on it. A Lucian code.

PYHR ZBIRQ SBE FNSRXRRCVAT
KEY: OFFSET 13

He sighed but then took a deep breath and turned around. "That's all right, boy. We'll find it eventually." He grinned. "Let's go cheer ourselves up by terrifying some Germans." He reached behind him and gave the lion a pat. "I heard the Red Baron is afraid of cats." ✣

GERVAIS RAOUL LUFBERY (1885–1918)

Gervais Raoul Lufbery had three qualities guaranteed to make any Cahill a top Clue hunter. . . .

He was a citizen of both America and France, which gave him access to twice the Clue locations.

He was an ace fighter pilot.

And he had two pet lions.

Lufbery was born in France to an American father and a French mother. His father was a chemist who worked at a chocolate company during the day and performed secret Clue-related research at night.

At the start of World War I, Lufbery signed up for pilot training and joined the French Air Service. A true Janus, Lufbery turned flying into an art with his bold style and daring moves. He shot down a record number of enemy planes, earning the title of "flying ace."

When he wasn't busy flying circles around his opponents, Lufbery used his pilot skills to look for Clues in Europe, which is why he was sometimes spotted far from the battlefields. Agents from other branches knew better than to interfere with Lufbery's missions. Not only did he have deadly aim, but he kept two lion cubs as pets—Whiskey and Soda—and they often accompanied him on these special trips for protection. Tragically, Lufbery was shot down and killed before the end of the war, but he remains one of the most revered agents in Janus history.

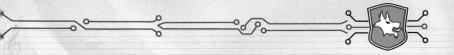

WOLFGANG AMADEUS MOZART (1756–1791)

Wolfgang Amadeus Mozart is considered history's greatest musician. Mozart's father, Leopold, was a Janus agent desperate to break into his branch's inner circle. When his young children, Wolfang and Nannerl, showed signs of musical genius, he realized that they could gain him entry into that world.

Leopold arranged for Wolfgang and Nannerl to perform all over Europe, including Germany, France, England, and Italy. He eventually decided to focus his attention on Wolfgang and soon established him as one of the most talented young musicians in Europe.

As an adult, Mozart wrote over 600 pieces of music, including 41 symphonies and several operas, such as *The Marriage of Figaro* and *The Magic Flute*. A true Janus, Mozart was constantly creating. There are reports of him writing music while speaking to friends and even while playing billiards.

Mozart also grew up to become a devoted Clue hunter. He was obsessed with re-creating the Janus serum and fantasized about the musical revolution he could lead with this extra boost of talent. However, tracking down Clues turned out to be an expensive quest. Mozart died penniless and was buried in an unmarked grave. Over the years, the plots in Vienna's St. Marx cemetery were rearranged, and Mozart's body was lost. To this day, no one is quite sure where his bones lie.

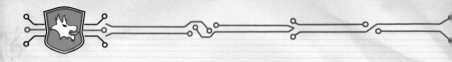

HARRY HOUDINI (1874–1926)

Most people might not consider climbing out of a milk can to be art. However, Janus agent Harry Houdini was a genius at turning his talent for escape into a stunning spectacle. He dazzled crowds by completing stunts while handcuffed, or bound by a straitjacket, or even while being suspended from the ceiling by his feet.

As his dangerous stunts turned him into an international celebrity, Houdini used fame as an excuse to travel the world . . . and go on secret Clue-hunting missions. With his talent for lock picking and his ability to escape from any situation, Houdini was the Janus's first choice for important—and potentially deadly—tasks.

Yet as Houdini's stunts grew more extreme, the other branches began to grow suspicious. After he escaped from a Russian prison van headed for Siberia, the Lucians realized that Houdini was on the hunt for one of their Clues. They sent two men to pose as fans and challenge Houdini to prove one of his claims—that he could withstand any blow to the abdomen. According to most reports, one of the men punched Houdini before he was prepared, causing serious organ damage. Houdini fell ill after the encounter and died a few days later.

However, the Janus always believed that the Lucians poisoned Houdini. In 2007, his great-nephew petitioned to exhume Houdini's body so it could be reexamined, but Lucian lawmakers blocked the request. They prefer their handiwork to remain a secret.

JANUS
AGENTS

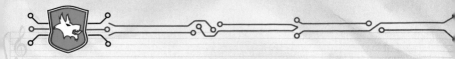

The other Cahills tend to underestimate the Janus, questioning whether someone can be both an artist and a fearsome Clue hunter. The Janus enjoy proving their rivals wrong by sending top agents into the field such as Maria Marapao, a poet and a champion martial artist. Like many Janus agents, Maria is a highly trained Clue hunter who can defuse a bomb in the same time it takes her to write a haiku. The top agents include:

JONAH WIZARD   SOPHIE WATSON
CORA WIZARD   LAN NGUYEN
BRODERICK WIZARD   OPHIR DHUPAM
STEVEN SPIELBERG   LESLIE D. MILL
JUSTIN BIEBER   DANIEL RADCLIFFE

CORA WIZARD

Cora Wizard is a world-famous artist. After becoming the youngest person ever to win the Nobel Prize in Literature, she switched her focus to painting. She's spent the past few years traveling, displaying her work in the most prestigious galleries. But only Cahill insiders know the real reason for Cora's jet-setting—as the head of the Janus branch, she had to visit strongholds and bases to oversee Janus Clue-hunting efforts around the world. Sometimes, Cora's travel plans coincided with her son's tour schedule. At those concerts, Jonah would always scan the VIP section for his mother, but she never came. However, he knows better than to

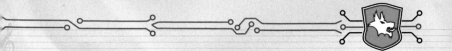

look for her now. After Jonah shared his Clues in the Madrigal stronghold, Cora vowed never to speak to him again.

SOPHIE WATSON

Sophie Watson is the daughter of the two highest-ranking Janus agents in London. They agreed to send Sophie to the same school as Natalie Kabra so she could spy on their Lucian rival. Natalie spends a great deal of time mocking Sophie's creative clothes and her experimental dance performances, but she has no idea that Sophie hacked into her school e-mail account and reads her messages every day. Sophie doesn't mind that Natalie makes fun of her. She gets the last laugh when she forwards top secret information from Isabel Kabra to the Janus leadership.

LAN NGUYEN

Lan grew up in Melbourne, Australia, the daughter of two retired Janus who wanted to raise their children apart from the madness of the Clue hunt. However, when Lan discovered her family's secret history, she became committed to the Janus cause. She heard about a Clue hidden somewhere in India and traveled thousands of miles from home to track it down. When Cora Wizard

learned about Lan's accomplishments, she invited Lan to the
Hollywood stronghold for
advanced training. Today,
she's considered one of
the most promising young
agents in the branch.

LESLIE D. MILL

Leslie D. Mill is a
Hollywood director and an
active Janus agent. When
Cora Wizard learned that
there was a lost Ekat Clue
connected to Nikola Tesla,
she ordered Leslie to start
production on a movie
about the famous inven-
tor. That way, the Janus
would be given permission to explore important sites as part of
their "location scouting." However, the film was never completed.
Cora and Leslie's "artistic differences" caused them to fight about
everything from the casting to the costumes. As a result, Cora
chose a different director for her next project—a movie about the
life of Josephine Baker.

OPHIR DHUPAM

Ophir is a superstar in the Indian film industry. However,
he's not content with the love of his millions of fans—he wants
to prove himself to his fellow Janus by finding more Clues than
any other agent. He even arranged to film a movie about the

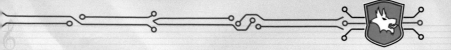

life of Shah Jahan in order to snoop around the Taj Mahal. However, Ophir's efforts didn't quite pay off. The Clue was revealed to be in another monument: the Red Fort in Delhi.

BRODERICK WIZARD

Broderick was not born into the Janus branch. He only learned about the Cahills and the Clues after he married Cora. Even after seventeen years of marriage, there are secrets Cora refuses to share with her husband—he doesn't have the necessary security clearance. However, as Jonah's manager, Broderick had plenty to keep him busy apart from the Clue hunt. Cora had little interest in their superstar son's dazzling career, so she left it up to Broderick. Touring with Jonah was the only time when Broderick got to make decisions on his own—a rare thing for a non-Janus living with one of the most powerful women on earth. However, everything changed after the Clue hunt. Cora disowned Jonah and, after years of following Cora's lead, Broderick took a stand. His chose his son over his wife.

POSSIBLE HEIST TIMES

1:30   12:00   6:30   4:00   9:00

12:00   9:30   12:00   8:30

3:00   2:00   9:30

JONAH WIZARD

AGE: 15
BRANCH: JANUS
HOMETOWN:
LOS ANGELES, USA

AGENT UPDATE: Jonah Wizard

"I'm Jonah Wizard. Welcome to my crib." Jonah tried to smile at the camera but, after eight takes, his cheeks were starting to hurt.

"That was better," called Lisa, the producer of MTV's *Cribs*. "But can you lose the cast for the next take? It's not really, you know, part of your whole 'gangsta' image."

Jonah glanced down at the plaster cast that extended from his ankle to the top of his thigh. After leaving the Madrigal stronghold, he'd flown straight to London, where he'd undergone an eight-hour surgery to stabilize his shattered leg.

"No, not really," he said. "Unless you want to come back in three months."

"Well, hmm." Lisa frowned. "Can you at least tell the viewers how you got hurt?" Her eyes widened. "I got it. You were rapping on top of an elephant when all these screaming fans showed up and the elephant, like, took off running." She paused. "It should probably be a rare albino elephant." She turned to her headphone-wearing assistant. "Go see if we can Photoshop him onto one."

"Hold up," Jonah said. "I'm not down with lying to my fans."

Lisa stared at him for a moment. "Okaaay. So, what really happened?"

Jonah imagined what would happen if he told Lisa the truth. *I'm actually a member of the most powerful family in history, and I was on the hunt for these 39 Clues. . . .* Yeah. That would go over well.

"It's a boring story," Jonah said. "But," he continued after Lisa's face fell. "I became the first person to accept a Kids' Choice Award from an intensive care unit."

Lisa nodded. "That *is* pretty gangsta. Okay. Let's roll the cameras!"

Three hours later, Jonah was beginning to regret buying such a big house. It was getting late, and he still hadn't shown the crew the recording studio or indoor go-kart track. He glanced down at his phone. Four missed calls. As he scrolled through the caller ID, he felt his stomach tighten. All Boston phone numbers. He'd have to wait for the MTV crew to leave before he could figure out what was going on.

They were in the library, an ultramodern room that took up half of the third floor. It had been Jonah's main reason for choosing the mansion. That, and the sprawling backyard with space for the crocodile habitat he'd installed. The paparazzi would think twice before sneaking onto his property.

Lisa was scurrying around the room, pointing out features to the cameraman. "This is *awesome*," she shouted from the balcony. "So it's just you and your parents who live here?"

A series of images flashed through Jonah's mind. Broderick's new king-sized bed with its single pillow. The sparse bathroom without any makeup or jewelry in sight. A dining room table that wasn't covered with his mother's half-finished sketches. He inhaled. Who would've thought he'd ever miss the smell of acrylic paint?

He flashed Lisa a well-practiced grin. "Yeah. It's just the three of us." He turned away before she noticed that his smile didn't reach his eyes.

Right before they began shooting, Jonah's phone buzzed again. He tensed as he felt the vibration.

Lisa hurried over to Jonah. "OK, I think we're ready to start. Ready, Chloe?" she shouted to the host of MTV's *Cribs*. Jonah sighed. Chloe had been all over him ever since she'd found out he was producing a hip-hop version of *Romeo and Juliet*. She thought TV was a waste of her "talent" and was ready to break into film.

"Ready!" Chloe called as she teetered over in her stilettos.

"Okay," said Lisa. "Roll camera."

"So, Jonah," Chloe began as she wobbled toward the bookcase. "Tell us about this library. Do you read a lot?"

Jonah paused. He thought back to his conversation with Mrs. Pluderbottom in England, when he'd tried to hide his love of Shakespeare. It felt like a lifetime ago. He turned to Chloe. "Yeah. I read all the time."

Her large eyes widened even more. "Really? How intriguing." She batted her eyelashes and tried to take a step toward Jonah, but her heels sank into the thick carpet and she had to grab on to a chair to keep from falling down. "I guess that explains all the books." She turned and began running her fingers along the spines. "Oooh, this one's pretty," she said, stopping on a purple clothbound book with gold lettering. "*Love's Labour's Won*."

"Don't touch that!" Jonah yelped, limping over to her.

"Why not?" Chloe frowned. "Was it a present from a girl? Do you have a girlfriend? Is she an actress?" she asked. Her voice was getting rather shrill.

"No," Jonah answered, removing her hand from the book. "It's just, um, really old."

Chloe nodded gravely. "I get it. I have an issue of *Vogue* from 1976 in mint condition."

Jonah flashed her his famous smile. "Sounds dope, yo. Come on, let's go check out the spa."

After the crew had finally finished packing their equipment, Jonah hobbled back up to the library. By the time he reached the bookcase, he was out of breath.

Next time, I'll trade the sneaker room for an elevator.

He glanced around, even though he knew he was alone in the house. Broderick was meeting with Jonah's lawyer. And Cora was . . . well, Jonah wasn't sure where his mother was. He hadn't seen her since he'd returned to America.

He grabbed the top of the purple book Chloe had been examining earlier, *Love's Labour's Won*, and pulled. There was a clicking noise and the bookcase swung open to reveal a metal door. He typed a code into the keypad and the door rose up.

Jonah made his way carefully down the stairs. If he tripped and fell, no one would be able to find him. When he reached the bottom, he pressed a button on the wall and heard the metal door lower. A few moments later, he heard the soft *thump* of the bookcase swinging back into place.

Jonah flipped on the lights and looked around the room. It was completely soundproof. No one would ever overhear him practicing new songs or—his eyes passed over the enormous flat-screen monitor on the wall—having top secret conversations. He limped over and pressed his hand against the screen. It glowed and the words "four missed video calls" appeared. Underneath it read:

15:24	Amy Cahill
16:07	Dan Cahill
17:12	William McIntyre
17:23	Dan Cahill

He pressed the speech bubble icon next to Amy's name to play her voice mail. "Jonah," Amy's panicked voice blared out from the speakers. There was a lot of static in the background. "It's me. Dan and I are in Switzerland. We went to Grace's bank and—" There was a muffled sound. Jonah couldn't tell if it was static or a sob. "They found us."

She gasped. "The Vespers are coming."

JANUS
TRICKS & TOOLS

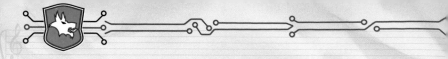

The Janus excel at mixing business with pleasure. Most of their Clue-hunting strategies involve creating art. Whether by hiding codes in sheet music or filming a movie in known Cahill hot spots, the Janus's sneakiest missions are always performed with style. Their favorite tricks and tools include:

MUSIC CODES
IMPERSONATIONS
CAMOUFLAGE
HIDING MESSAGES IN ART
LIBRARY CODES
DISGUISES
SURVEILLANCE VANS
CLUE-INSPIRED FILMS

IMPERSONATIONS

With their talent for acting and designing costumes, the Janus have long used impersonation as a Clue-hunting tactic. In the late 18th century, the Janus learned that a Tomas Clue had been brought to France. There were rumors that it was connected to a large diamond set to become part of the crown jewels. In an attempt to intercept the diamond before it was delivered to the royal court, the Janus sent an actress dressed as Marie Antoinette to the jewelers. Although the plan ultimately failed, it showed the Janus the usefulness of skilled impersonators.

When Cora Wizard desperately needed a document she knew was hidden in the Lucian stronghold in Paris, she came up with a brilliant plan. She found a Janus actress to impersonate Isabel Kabra. After a few weeks of preparation, the actress had Isabel's voice and mannerisms down pat, from her posh accent to the terrifying eyebrow raise that generally comes right before an

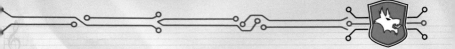

execution order. The actress's mission was a success. The only downside is that now Cora is on Isabel's lengthy "to kill" list.

HIDING MESSAGES IN ART

For centuries, the Janus have used books, paintings, sculptures, and buildings to hide Clues and hints—such as the Clue hidden in Mary Shelley's novel *Frankenstein*. To the untrained eye, Janus masterpieces seem to be beautiful works of art, but many of them contain crucial information. Most of Cora Wizard's paintings contain messages to her top agents, from the location of the next leadership meeting to the Cahill at the top of her "most wanted" list. At the moment, it's Isabel Kabra, for what she did to Cora's son. Cora may not be speaking to Jonah currently, but no one is allowed to mess with a Wizard except Cora herself.

SPY PIGEONS

The Janus creativity allows them to come up with crazy— and very effective—Clue-hunting tools. For centuries, humans have used pigeons to send messages. In World War I, a brave carrier pigeon, Cher Ami, was even awarded the Croix de Guerre medal after delivering a message that saved the lives of almost 200 trapped soldiers. However, the Janus were the first to equip pigeons with cameras to take spy photos of important Clue locations, whether enemy strongholds or

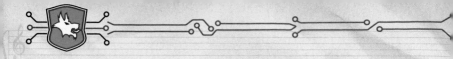

their own bases. When the other branches learned that there might be a Clue hidden in Neuschwanstein Castle, the Janus dispatched fleets of spy pigeons to photograph the area and monitor their enemies' movements.

CLUE-INSPIRED FILMS

The Cahills spend billions of dollars a year spying on each other, which makes it hard for the branches to protect their secrets. However, the Janus branch has a strategy for making sure no one learns about their Clue-hunting missions. Whenever they want to investigate a suspected Clue location, they simply arrange to shoot a movie there. The other branches monitor all Hollywood film productions for this reason, but they always have trouble figuring out which projects are real and which are covers. Janus actor Ophir Dhupam had nearly completed shooting his movie about Shah Jahan before the other branches discovered the *real* reason for his interest in the Taj Mahal.

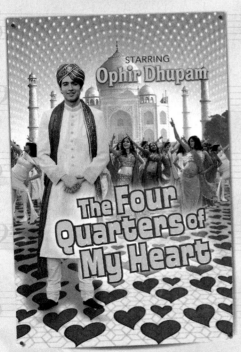

STARRING
Ophir Dhupam

The Four Quarters of My Heart

JANUS
HOT SPOTS

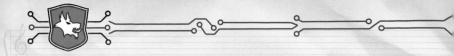

Just because a stronghold needs to be ultrasecure and completely secret, doesn't mean it has to be ugly. At least, that's been the Janus philosophy for the past 500 years. They've established bases in the some of the most beautiful cities on earth and have used some of the world's most famous buildings to protect Clues. However, their passion for art doesn't make the Janus any less sneaky than their Cahill rivals. They might have chosen the Hagia Sophia for its gorgeous mosaics, but it also proved to be an ideal hiding place. For the past three centuries, no one has been able to find the Clue inside the former church. Janus bases around the world include:

MONTREAL, CANADA

TAJ MAHAL, INDIA

BUDAPEST, HUNGARY

HOLLYWOOD, USA

LA SAGRADA FAMILIA, SPAIN

HAGIA SOPHIA, TURKEY

NEUSCHWANSTEIN CASTLE, GERMANY

ROANOKE, USA

VIENNA, AUSTRIA

RED FORT, INDIA

ROME, ITALY

VENICE, ITALY

LISBON, PORTUGAL

VENICE

One of the main Janus strongholds is in Venice, Italy. It's a vast, hidden underground complex that contains artist studios, galleries, and meeting spaces, as well as storage rooms for the countless number of priceless Janus masterpieces. Agents with top clearance can admire secret paintings by van Gogh or read the Jane Austen novel that was written exclusively for her fellow Janus. The stronghold's advanced security system makes it ideal for hiding Clues and confidential Clue-related evidence, like the crucial missing pages from Nannerl Mozart's diary.

HOLLYWOOD

The Janus have been a major presence in Hollywood since the birth of the film industry in the 1910s, gaining fame as actors, writers, directors, costume designers, and more. Most of the notable names in entertainment have belonged to the Janus branch, including Marlon Brando, Marilyn Monroe, Charlie Chaplin, Steven Spielberg, and Daniel Radcliffe. Because so many Janus live and work in the Los Angeles area, they built their main stronghold underneath the Hollywood sign in the Hollywood hills. The entrance is inside one of the letter "O's." In order to gain access, agents must stand in front of the hidden retina scanner. Then, to ensure that the visitor isn't an eyeball-stealing imposter, he or she must answer a question about Janus history, such as the name of Mary Shelley's unpublished sequel to *Frankenstein*. If the agent responds correctly, a panel in the "O" slides open, revealing a secret elevator.

TAJ MAHAL

Janus architect Ustad Lahauri designed the Taj Mahal, one of the most famous buildings in the world, at the request of Emperor

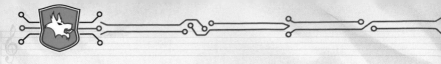

Shah Jahan in honor of his deceased wife. For centuries, there were rumors that Lahauri hid a Clue inside the Taj Mahal but, in recent years, top Cahill agents discovered that the Clue was actually inside another one of Lahauri's monuments—the Red Fort in Delhi.

NEUSCHWANSTEIN CASTLE

One of King Ludwig's many fantasy palaces, Neuschwanstein Castle featured lavish bedrooms, concert halls, dining rooms— even an indoor grotto with an artificial waterfall. Cahill insiders always suspected that Ludwig was hiding a Clue in one of his palaces but, even after his death, none of the other branches ever found his supersecret hiding place. The Clue remained safe in Neuschwanstein's grotto for centuries.

HAGIA SOPHIA

During the height of Janus power in Turkey, the branch decided to hide a Clue in the Hagia Sophia, a church that was transformed into a mosque before becoming a museum. The building was perfect. The ornate decorations satisfied the Janus need for beauty and made it easy to hide a tiny Clue hint—the alchemical sign for lead.

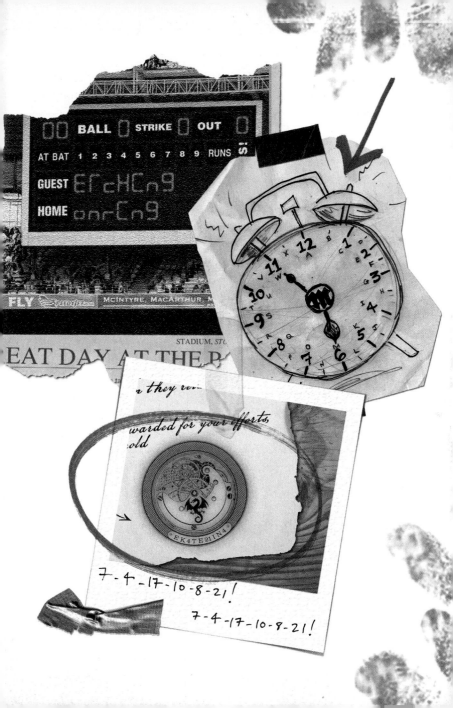

Speedy Monkey

For Joshua Comyn with love x
– Jeanne

To all the wonderful animals in the world
– Chantelle and Burgen

STRIPES PUBLISHING LTD
An imprint of the Little Tiger Group
1 Coda Studios, 189 Munster Road, London SW6 6AW

First published in Great Britain in 2019.

Text copyright © Jeanne Willis, 2019
Illustrations © Chantelle and Burgen Thorne, 2019

ISBN: 978-1-78895-114-2

Printed and bound in China.

STP/1800/0264/0419

2 4 6 8 10 9 7 5 3 1

Speedy Monkey

Jeanne Willis

Illustrated by Chantelle and Burgen Thorne

STRIPES

Deep in the rainforest, all was peaceful,
all was calm.

The river ran slowly, Sloth snored softly and
Jaguar slipped through the undergrowth on
his padded paws, silent as a shadow.

But then…

1

Along came Speedy Monkey!

From the day he was born in the Brazil Nut Tree, Speedy just couldn't keep still and he couldn't keep quiet. Why should he? Why would he? He was young and bright and full of curiosity.

"Wheeeeeee!"

All day long, he chattered to himself...

What's this?

What's that?

Why?

He never stopped questioning
and wondering.

When?

Where?

Who?

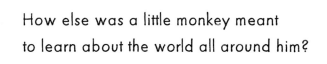

How else was a little monkey meant
to learn about the world all around him?

Speedy's fiddly fingers never stopped
fidgeting – they were perfect for flicking
and picking, scratching and catching and
poking into everyone's business. His twiddly
toes grabbed and gripped and stopped him
slipping when he climbed ... and how he
loved to climb!

He would whizz to the top of the
Wumba Tree with a loud WHOOP,
startling Chameleon and waking
Snake.

Then he'd hang upside down by his
curly, twirly tail and ...

swiiiiiiiiiiiiiiiing!

Backwards and forwards, looping the
loop, looking for someone, anyone to
join in with his games.

Hoping that today was the day he might find a friend to play with, he gave an ear-splitting

"WOO-HOO!"

and did a daring LEAP over Lizard.

He landed right on top of
Toucan who almost toppled
off his branch.

"Let's play bouncing, Toucan!" he yelled.
"Hold on tight!"

"Can't you sit still for five minutes?" moaned
Toucan.

"What's five?
What's a minute?
What's sitting still?"

asked Speedy. "I have never tried it."

"Try now," begged Toucan. "Sit on your
bottom nicely and watch the world go by
with me."

Speedy sat next to him on the
branch and did his very best
to stay still.

But after one minute, his fingers
twitched. After two minutes,
his toes itched. After three
minutes, he couldn't stand
sitting still for a second longer.
He stood up and bounced so
hard, he catapulted Toucan
right into the sky.

"I don't want to watch
the world go by. I want
to keep up with it!" said
Speedy. "Come back,
Toucan!"

But Toucan had flown
away.

Then Speedy
spotted some fallen fruit on
the forest floor. He was busy juggling
with it when he almost tripped over
something. At first he thought it was a
stone, but when he looked closer, he saw
that whatever it was had stumpy legs
and a tiny tail at the back. "Ooh,
who are you?" he said.

There was no reply, so he went round
to look at the front and saw two scaly
arms and a little bald head with
nostrils the size of pin holes.

"Excuse me, where are your eyes?"
said Speedy. "Are you asleep?
What happens if I do this?" and he
tickled the creature under the chin.

With a startled hiss, Red-Footed Tortoise
pulled his head into his shell along with
his arms and legs.

"Where have you gone? What are you
doing? Cooeee!" called Speedy.

Tortoise huffed and poked
his head out. For some reason,
he seemed rather annoyed.

"You made me jump!" he said.
"I was trying to sunbathe."

"Why?" said Speedy.

"It's what reptiles do," said Tortoise.
"We bask in the sun."

"Why?" said Speedy. "How often?"

Tortoise gave a deep sigh.
"Too many questions," he said,
retreating into his shell.
"Now, if you don't mind,
I'm going back indoors.
Please leave quietly."

But Speedy didn't
understand "quietly".
All day long,

he whooped

and
swooped,

pranced

and danced,

and
jumped

and thumped.

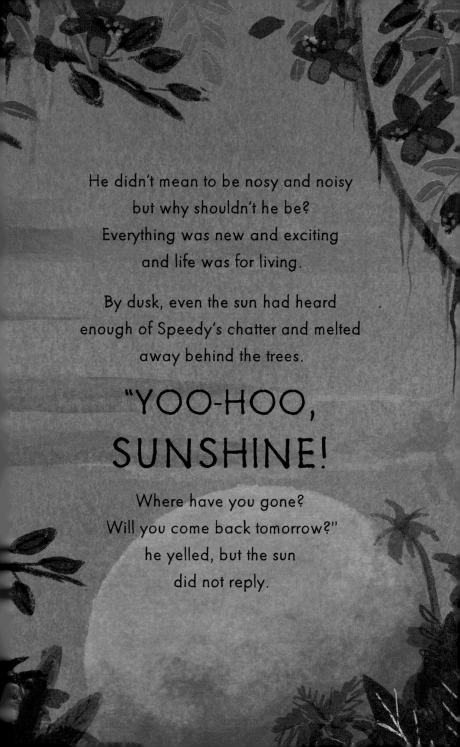

He didn't mean to be nosy and noisy
but why shouldn't he be?
Everything was new and exciting
and life was for living.

By dusk, even the sun had heard
enough of Speedy's chatter and melted
away behind the trees.

"YOO-HOO,
SUNSHINE!

Where have you gone?
Will you come back tomorrow?"
he yelled, but the sun
did not reply.

Darkness fell
and as the moon rose,
the daytime animals went home
to their nooks and nests and niches
and tried to sleep.
But somebody wasn't tired.
Not in the slightest!
Speedy was still wide awake and
he went swinging through the stars,
singing at the top of his voice,

"One banana,
two bananas
hanging on the tree,
three bananas
four bananas,
come and play
with me!"

"Give it a rest!" roared Jaguar.

"You've woken me up!"
squawked Scarlet Macaw.

"Hushhhhhhh!" hissed Anaconda.

But Speedy couldn't rest or sleep
or hush. How could he? The night
was full of magical sights, mystical
sounds and mysterious smells.
He wanted to see and sense and
sniff them all, because the night
was young and so was he.

29

Soon, even the night animals
had had enough of him.
By nature they were quiet,
shy, polite creatures and felt
uncomfortable with anyone who
wasn't the same. They liked to
keep themselves to themselves
and loud noises and sudden
movements frightened them.

Speedy didn't understand.
He didn't know why Gecko
ran off or why Ant Eater turned
tail or why Armadillo curled
into a tight ball when he tried
to play with them. He was
born a monkey and behaved
like a monkey — he just
couldn't help it.

Happily for Speedy, Sloth — who was slower than everybody at everything — was much slower to tell Speedy off for causing a commotion. He simply didn't have the energy.

"I ... say," he said wearily, as he dangled from a branch by his long, curved claws.

"What do you say?" chattered Speedy, racing up the tree and jigging up and down.

"I ... say," repeated Sloth even more slowly. "Isn't it...?"

"Isn't it what?" asked Speedy, trying to hurry Sloth along. "Isn't it time we dive-bombed into the river? Isn't it time we went roly poly, roly poly down the hill?"

Sloth shook his head. "No. Isn't it time you—?" but Speedy was so excited he interrupted Sloth again.

"Isn't it time I chased you round the Cashew Tree? Isn't it time I showed you my cheeky dance?"

Sloth shuffled a few millimetres backwards.
It took him ten minutes, by which time Speedy
was desperate to know what he had to say.
Finally, Sloth took a deep breath and this time,
he almost managed to get to the end of his
sentence. "Isn't it ... time you ... went to...?"

"Climb that mountain?

Catch that star?

Touch the moon?"
guessed Speedy.

"No..." muttered Sloth. "What I'm trying to say is — isn't it time you went to sleep?"

Speedy's face fell. "Sleep?" he said. "Why would I want to sleep when I'm wide awake?"

"I always do," Sloth replied.

"But I'm not a sloth," said Speedy.

Sloth closed his eyes. "You could pretend to be one," he said. "Then we could be friends."

Speedy really wanted a friend, so he agreed — he would pretend to be a sloth. "What do I have to do?" he asked.

"Just copy me," said Sloth.

Speedy hung upside down from the branch just
like Sloth, who didn't move or speak for ages.
By now Speedy was feeling restless, but he
was so keen to be the perfect sloth, he tried
his best not to fidget. "Now what should I do?"
he asked.

Sloth blinked at him in surprise. "Nothing, of
course," he replied.

"Nothing?" said Speedy, who had never done
nothing in his life. "But that's boring."

Sloth looked most insulted. "Doing nothing
means everything to a sloth," he said.
"If you can't grasp that simple rule, there's not
much point in us hanging out together."

Speedy was surprised to hear that, but then
he had a brilliant idea.

"I'm not very good at being a sloth," he said, "but we
could be friends if you pretended to be a monkey.

It's such fun! We could leap like Frog, run rings round Rat and blow raspberries at Warthog. Say you will, Sloth … Sloth?"

But Sloth was sound asleep.

Speedy swung from tree to tree, calling and
searching for someone else to play with, but
no one wanted to join in with his crazy capers.

"Keep the noise down, you!" said Kinkajou.

"Quiet! I'm trying to think!" said Skink.

"Off you trot!" said Ocelot.

40

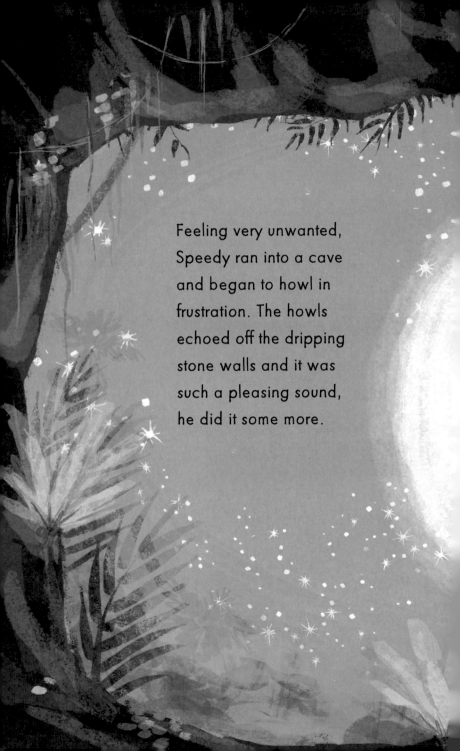

Feeling very unwanted, Speedy ran into a cave and began to howl in frustration. The howls echoed off the dripping stone walls and it was such a pleasing sound, he did it some more.

Howl Howl
Howl
Howl Howl...
Howl
Howl Howl
Howl...

43

"Stop that!" squeaked Bat.
"Why can't you be more like me
and stop bothering everybody?"

"I would if I could and I know I
should, but I'm not a bat!" howled
Speedy. "I'm a monkey, and I was
born to jump and swing and shout
'Woo-hoo!'"

"Hmm," said Bat. "If that's what
you were born to do, perhaps you
should go and do it somewhere
else. Everyone will love you for it."

"Will they?" said Speedy. "I would
like that very much!"

"Then I suggest you take yourself off
to the far edge of the forest, climb
to the tip top of the Kapok Tree and
be as loud as you want," she said.

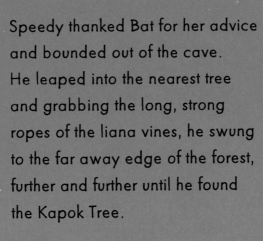

Speedy thanked Bat for her advice
and bounded out of the cave.
He leaped into the nearest tree
and grabbing the long, strong
ropes of the liana vines, he swung
to the far away edge of the forest,
further and further until he found
the Kapok Tree.

It stood alone in a clearing
like a giant king, towering
above the other trees that
bowed down before it.

Speedy had never seen a tree
that tall before.

He climbed and he climbed,
paw over paw, foot over foot,
using his tail to keep his balance.

Higher and higher he went until
he could almost touch the stars.

Finally he reached the top.
Feeling very pleased with himself,
he bounced up and down on
the highest, whippiest branch,
whooping and shrieking in triumph,
but to his great astonishment,
nobody told him to be quiet.

"That's odd." He frowned. "I'll try being noisier and see if anyone minds that!"

Speedy whistled and called and screeched and clapped. He bashed and crashed and smashed and slapped. But still nobody said a word.

"Bat was right to send me here!" He smiled. "I'm being louder than ever, yet no one is telling me off. It must mean that everybody loves me as I am now. This must be a magic tree that makes everyone like monkeys!"

But Speedy was wrong.
It wasn't a magic tree.
The only reason no one had told him
to be quiet was because nobody
was there to hear him.
The other animals never came
to this part of the forest.
Bat knew that, but Speedy didn't.

"Yoo-hoo! Come and play with me!"
he called.

There was no reply.

"Perhaps they can't hear me
because I'm so high up," he thought.
"Bat told me to go to the top of the tree,
but if I dangle by my long tail,
I'll be a little lower."

Speedy hung upside down and
he swung to and fro, hollering loudly.

"Hello?

Hello?"

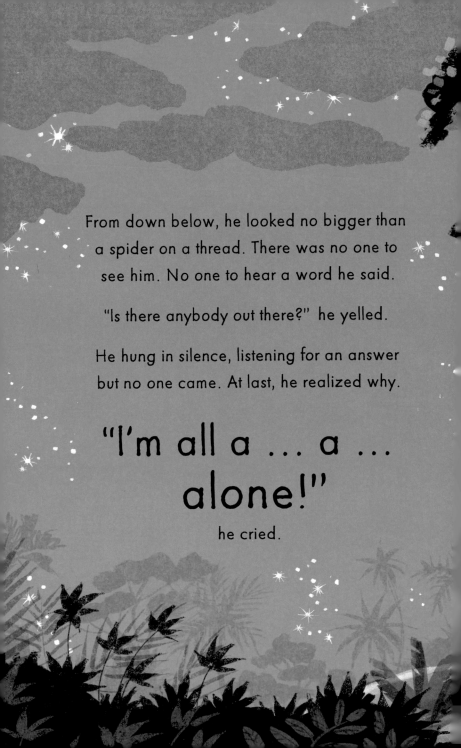

From down below, he looked no bigger than a spider on a thread. There was no one to see him. No one to hear a word he said.

"Is there anybody out there?" he yelled.

He hung in silence, listening for an answer but no one came. At last, he realized why.

"I'm all a ... a ... alone!"

he cried.

55

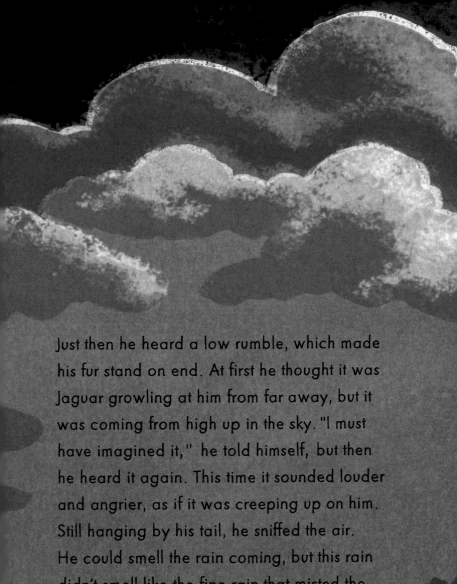

Just then he heard a low rumble, which made
his fur stand on end. At first he thought it was
Jaguar growling at him from far away, but it
was coming from high up in the sky. "I must
have imagined it," he told himself, but then
he heard it again. This time it sounded louder
and angrier, as if it was creeping up on him.
Still hanging by his tail, he sniffed the air.
He could smell the rain coming, but this rain
didn't smell like the fine rain that misted the
leaves with tiny silver beads. This rain smelled
electric. The air began to fizz.

Suddenly, a zigzag of fire ripped through
the darkness. Speedy almost fell out of the
Kapok Tree. He grabbed the branch with
both hands and swung himself up.

The rain fell in heavy drops that stung
his nose. The wind whistled in his ears.
The tree began to buck and sway like
a ship tossed by enormous waves.
A terrible storm was brewing!

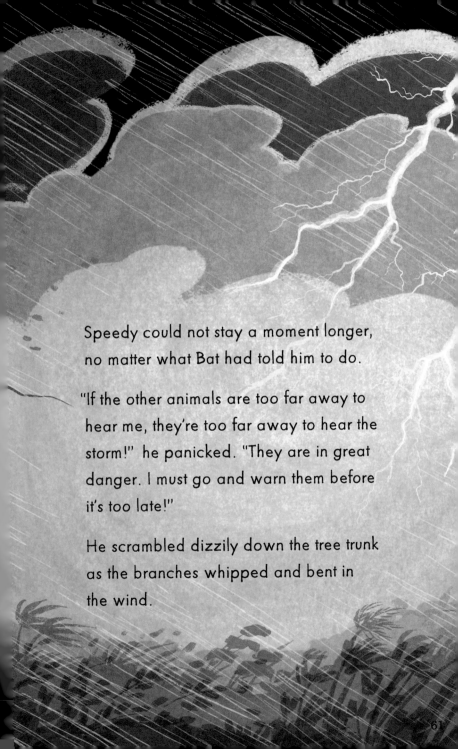

Speedy could not stay a moment longer, no matter what Bat had told him to do.

"If the other animals are too far away to hear me, they're too far away to hear the storm!" he panicked. "They are in great danger. I must go and warn them before it's too late!"

He scrambled dizzily down the tree trunk as the branches whipped and bent in the wind.

"Storm!"

he screamed, over the thunder.

"Storm coming! Run for your lives!"

Speedy leaped and swung faster than he
had ever done in his life, saying to himself,
"I must outrun the storm to reach them in time.
I must shout louder than thunder to make
myself heard!" If he failed, the forest would be
flattened before the night creatures had time
to escape. The day creatures would wake to
find themselves trapped by fallen trees, and
those who could not fly or swim would be
washed away in the flood.

Speedy raced around the thick canopy of leaves
that circled the forest to warn Toucan and Sloth.
"Wake up! Wake up!"
he yelled.

"What's all the noise?" grumbled Toucan, his head still under his wing.

Speedy bounced up and down on the branch, waving his paws about to get their attention.

"The storm is coming!" he said. "Spread the word. You need to leave quickly!"

"Quickly?" mumbled Sloth. "Me?"

"Please, you must hurry like a monkey!" said Speedy. "Or you may not be a sloth for much longer. The storm is on my heels! Head for Bat's cave."

Feeling the first blast of wind, the canopy creatures fled through the night as Speedy swung down to the forest understorey to warn Jaguar and Tree Frog.

"Why aren't you in bed?" growled Jaguar.

"The storm is coming!" shrieked Speedy. "It'll be here any moment. Run! Hop away!"

"Storm?" croaked Tree Frog. "Is this one of your jokes? It's not even raining."

Just then, a heavy raindrop plopped on to Frog's head and almost flattened her.

"Storm's coming!" she gulped.
"Hold tight, tadpoles. Thanks
for the warning, Speedy!"

But Speedy had already gone.
He was running around the
forest floor trying to find Tortoise.
Finally he spotted him.

"I hope you haven't come to tickle me again," said Tortoise

"I've come to tell you a storm is coming!" cried Speedy.

"Nonsense," grumbled Tortoise. "I can't hear it... Arghh! What was that loud bang?"

"Thunder!"
said Speedy.

"Hurry to Bat's
cave, you will
be safe and dry
there. I would
carry you, but I
need to go and
warn Ant Eater."

Tortoise plodded
off as fast as he
could while Speedy
scurried away.

71

As the thunder roared outside
her cave, Bat wasn't prepared
for quite so many guests, but
they were welcome as long as
they behaved. Coming together
to survive the storm, the animals
put their differences aside.
Jaguar didn't stalk Warthog,
Anaconda didn't try to strangle
Sloth and Chameleon kept his
tongue to himself for once.

Everyone was friendly, calm and safe, but one thing worried Bat – there was no sign of Speedy. No one had seen him since he'd told them the storm was coming.

"He'll be fine," said Toucan.
"Won't he?"

"He'll be back, twice as fast and twice as loud," said Sloth hopefully.

"If he doesn't come home, I'll never forgive myself," said Bat. "I sent him to the far side of the forest to give us all a bit of peace and quiet, but I'd do anything to hear his voice now."

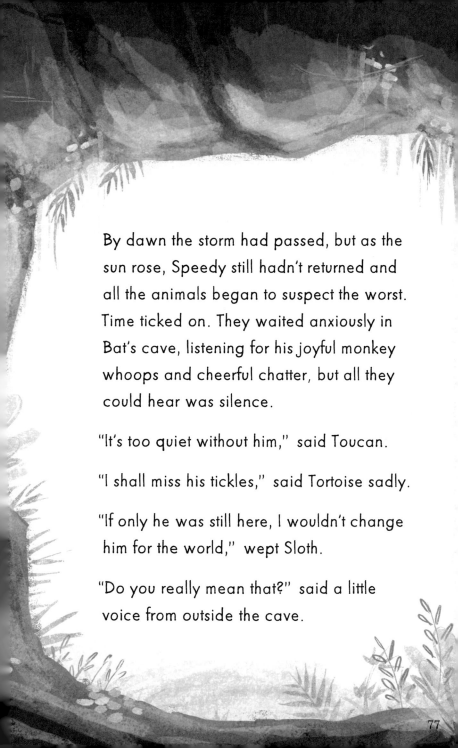

By dawn the storm had passed, but as the sun rose, Speedy still hadn't returned and all the animals began to suspect the worst. Time ticked on. They waited anxiously in Bat's cave, listening for his joyful monkey whoops and cheerful chatter, but all they could hear was silence.

"It's too quiet without him," said Toucan.

"I shall miss his tickles," said Tortoise sadly.

"If only he was still here, I wouldn't change him for the world," wept Sloth.

"Do you really mean that?" said a little voice from outside the cave.

"Speedy?" said Bat. "You're alive! Thank goodness! Where have you been?"

"Just playing quietly by myself," he said. "I thought that's what everyone wanted."

"Not any more!" they cried. "Your loudness and speed saved us from the storm. You're our hero!"

He gazed at them in surprise.
"Am I? Aren't I too loud? Too fast?"

The animals shook their heads.

"We love you just the way you are,"
said Bat.

"You do?" said Speedy.

"Yes," she said.
"And to thank you for being you, we're
going to have a party right now!"

Speedy rubbed his eyes
and gave a great big yawn.
"Now?" he said. "A party for me?
That's very kind but I'm afraid I'm much
too tired. I need to go to sleep,
so if you don't mind,
please would you keep
the noise down?"

The animals stared at each other in astonishment.

"Too tired?" said Jaguar.

"Go to sleep?" said Sloth.

"Keep the noise down?" said Toucan. "What happened to the wide-awake, fun-loving little monkey that we all know and love?"

Speedy's face split into an enormous grin. "Only joking! Here I am!" he said, and turning somersaults, he raced around Bat's cave, bouncing off the walls and shouting with joy.

83

And this time, everyone joined in.